The Scarlet Dusk

The Scarlet Dusk

Stories by
Saradindu Bandopadhyay

Translated by
Malobika Chaudhuri

Rupa & Co

Copyright © Prabir Chakraborty 2003
Translation Copyright © Malobika Chaudhuri 2003

Published by
Rupa . Co
7/16, Ansari Road, Daryaganj,
New Delhi 110 002

Sales Centres:

Allahabad Bangalore Chandigarh Chennai
Hyderabad Jaipur Kathmandu Kolkata
Ludhiana Mumbai Pune

All rights reserved.
No part of this publication may be reproduced, stored in a retrieval system, or transmitted, in any form or by any means, electronic, mechanical, photocopying, recording or otherwise, without the prior permission of the publishers.

Typeset 11 pts. ClassicalGaramond by
Nikita Overseas Pvt Ltd,
1410 Chiranjiv Tower,
43 Nehru Place
New Delhi 110 019

Printed in India by
Gopsons Papers Ltd.
A-14 Sector 60
Noida 201 301

Contents

The Scarlet Dusk	1
Incomparable	39
Why?	65
The Contrast	81
The Sandalwood Idol	97

The Scarlet Dusk

Sometimes, in a simple humdrum monotonous life, certain events take place like an earthquake, which when compared to the environment seems like an impossible disaster. The story which I am about to narrate today too appeared in my life unexpectedly, all of a sudden. Even though I had no contact with the story except as a spectator, it has left such a deep impression on my mind that it will probably remain indelible till the last days of my life.

It is seven days since since the man whose story I am recording today, departed for the Great Unknown, having been sentenced by the High Court. Hence, there is no means of bringing forth any proof or witnesses. But I will use all accounts published in the newspapers and all that the witnesses said during the course of the prisoner's trial and what is relevant to the story, as required. I do not ask anybody to believe me and there is no complaint either against those who scoff and want to disregard it as a figment of fanciful imagination. My only question is that, before death, instead of attempting in the least to gloss over his mistakes, why did a man have to lie so needlessly?

2 The Scarlet Dusk

First of all I am presenting an extract from a account of this incident that the daily newspaper 'Kalketu' had published at the time:

"Yesterday at almost 09.30 hrs a terrible murder took place in a butcher's shop on Durgacharn Banerjee Lane in Kolkata. Customarily, like all other days, the owner of the meat shop Gholam Quader was selling meat. Some Phiringis[1] and Muslim customers were present in the shop. In the meanwhile, another Phiringi wanted to purchase some beef. Immediately on seeing him, the owner Gholam Quader, with a terrible shriek pounced on him with the cleaver and inhumanly began stabbing him in the chest, stomach and face. When the victim fell to the ground, Gholam Quader climbed onto his chest and with each stab of the knife reiterated "Vasco da Gama, this is for my wife-this is for the daughter-this is for my aged father." Witnessing this hair-raising scene all those who were in the shop took to their heels and informed the police. When the police came and arrested Gholam Quader he was still sitting on the corpse, stabbing it and muttering as before.

One suspects that Gholam Quader suddenly lost his mind because it cannot be said that he had a previous acquaintance with the dead victim and neither is his wife, daughter and aged father alive at present. Investigations revealed that Gholam Quader was widowed almost fifteen years ago. His wife passed away, giving birth to a stillborn daughter. He has not remarried since.

---

1 **Phiringi:** Anglo-Indian, usually of European descent.

"According to police investigations, the dead man had recently newly arrived from Goa—a Portuguese Phiringi having come to Kolkata on business few days prior to that, he had put up in a small hotel. His name was Gabriel Deroza.

"Gholam Quader is now in custody. Deroza's corpse has been sent to the hospital for post-mortem."

My house was very close to the place where the incident had taken place and the entire episode interested me even more, because I had a nodding acquaintance with the man for a very long time. Besides which, another factor stirred my curiosity—that was the name of Vasco da Gama. I have been greatly enamoured with history ever since my childhood. 'Vasco da Gama' is not a commonly prevalent name; to find an illiterate Muslim butcher giving utterance to such a name and in such circumstances, the fragrance of some hidden romance stirred my soul. What strange mystery was cloistered in the folds of this ugly slaughter? Who was this Gabriel Deroza whom the murderer had addressed as 'Vasco da Gama'? Was it truly the rambling of an irresponsible madman?

Whatever that might be, my curiosity had grown to such an extent that the day this case came up in the Coroner's Court, I reached there early. The coroner had not reached but the accused had been brought in. Police were teeming all around. The accused was handcuffed and quietly seated on a tool. He recognized me and acknowledged with a 'salam'[2]. There seemed no sign of insanity-he appeared like an extremely easy-going human being. One could see no sign of fear or worry on his face. Who could say looking at him,

---

2 **Salam:** Respectful salutation.

that only two days ago he had so inhumanly slaughtered another man.

The coroner arrived and the proceedings began. The doctor was the first to take the stand. He said that that there was a total of fifty-seven stab wounds on the body. From these fifty-seven, it was difficult to pinpoint the exact one responsible for the death-because all were equally fatal.

After the Doctor had taken the witness stand, an Indian Christian named George Mathews was called. The witness said, following other questions and answers, "Since the past ten years I have been buying beef from Gholam Quader's shop almost every day; but never have I seen him react in this manner. By temperament he is a very quiet and polite man."

Quest-Do you think that at the time the dead man was attacked, he was not in his natural senses?

Ans-Till the dead man entered the shop he was perfectly normal-he was talking to us quite naturally; but the sight of Deroza seemed to turn him quite insane.

Quest-Did you have the impression that the accused knew the dead man prior to this?

Ans-Yes, but instead of calling him by the actual name, he had addressed him as 'Vasco da Gama'.

Quest-Did Deroza say anything when attacked?

Ans-No

Quest-Do you know if the accused drinks or indulges in any other sort of addiction?

Ans-I have never seen him indulging or getting drunk.

Quest-Did the accused by his demeanour indicate or give you the impression that he was murdering Deroza to fulfil a desire to take revenge?

The Scarlet Dusk 5

Ans-Yes. From what he said and his facial expressions, I had the impression that Deroza had previously tortured his wife, daughter and elderly father in some way.

Some more people following George Matthews took the witness stand and gave statements almost to the same effect. Then the Police Commissioner got up on the witness stand. He said that he had got word from Goa that Deroza was a petty businessman there, by nationality a Portuguese—aged forty two years. He had never left Goa and gone elsewhere prior to this and it was the first time he had stepped into Kolkata. About the accused the Police Commissioner said, "The accused does not have any relatives, wife or child. Investigations have revealed that in the past thirty years he has never left Kolkata. Hence it does not appear very likely that he had even met Deroza prior to this."

The accused had been standing quietly so far. Now he spoke, "I have seen Da Gama many times."

In an instant there was pin drop silence in the room. Signalling for the Deputy Commissioner to be quiet, the Coroner asked the accused, "Did you know Deroza previously?"

The accused said, "I have never seen Deroza—I know Vasco da Gama. In disguise, Vasco da Gama had come to my shop to purchase meat."

Casting a sharp glance at the accused, the Coroner said, "So, where have you seen Da Gama before?"

The accused responded, "The first time I saw him was at the port of Calicut and the last on the breast of the ocean," Saying this the accused abruptly stopped. I noticed that his face and eyes were turning red and he had difficulty in speaking. In a muffled voice he once cried out, "Ya Khuda[3]!" Then, hiding his face in his hands he sat down and did not speak another word.

Then in the course of time, the Coroner came up with the verdict that in a flash of momentary madness Gholam Quader had murdered Deroza.

When I emerged from the Court on the road outside, my head was spinning. 'Calicut', 'on the breast of the ocean'—what was all this that the accused had referred to? Who knows what he had further to say, what exquisite story lay buried in the illiterate and simple butcher, Gholam Quader's mind? It was obvious that he was not making any sort of pretence of madness. No talk or action of his remotely resembled that of a lunatic. Yet, through a couple of disjointed words, lifting an edge of the curtain of the past, what indication did he give of some astounding fairy tale?

After this, I see no necessity of giving details of all that happened in the life of Gholam Quader. Going through all the legal machinations, when the case was referred to the High Court, the Chief Justice ordered Gholam Quader to be kept under the strict supervision of a doctor for a month. After a month the doctor's report came in—Gholam Quader was a normal, simple man and there was no trace of madness in him. Then followed the judgement. During this, Gholam Quader, disregarding the advice of his lawyers clearly stated, "I have murdered and am not in the least bit sorry for it or regret it. If I were to meet him again, I would slaughter him in the same manner once more."

---

3 **Khuda:** God, as referred to by a Muslim.

Left with no choice the High Court ordered him to be hanged.

I was in the Court till the very last. In the drama of Gholam Quader's life, the Act of Judgement drew to a close—I sighed and came out. All through the Judgement, I had never expected freedom; but, even then, for no reason at all, a sadness overcame me. In some hidden corner of the heart a suspicion lingered that this was no fair judgement; somewhere, somehow, some urgent bit of evidence had been omitted.

As I was thinking about all this, some policemen brought the prisoner out. No sooner did I look at Gholam Quader's face, than he gestured for me to come close. Then, lowering his voice he said, "Babuji[4], you have been at my trial from the beginning to the very end—I have seen that myself. My time is up, but I have a last request—please come and meet me in jail once—I have something to say."

I said, "Definitely, I will do so."

Gholam Quader lifted his manacled hands in a namaskar[5] and getting into his jail car left.

A description of how I met him in jail after obtaining permission from the authorities is irrelevant here. All I am doing is translating in minute details the story narrated to me in the condemned prisoner's cell, just two days before his death.

Gholam Quader said, "Whether you believe this story of mine or not, at least do not disbelieve that I am not mad.

---

4 **Babuji:** A respectful form of address
5 **Namaskar:** A form of greeting with the palm of both hands folded together.

To tell the truth, this is also extremely strange to me. I have not read books and all my life have only sold meat. There is no capability in me to spin a tale. What I am about to tell you today I have experienced myself and so am able to describe it. But, that all these incidents did not take place in my that is this Gholam Quader's life, that is also definite. I do not know how I will get across to you, being an illiterate man. This much only I can affirm that it is not an incident taking place in the present, it happened a long, long time ago.

"Then, let me start at the very beginning. Fifteen-sixteen years ago my wife died giving birth to a girl and my daughter also died. Don't know how, but the idea became deeply rooted in my mind that my wife-child had been cruelly murdered. More than grief, a searing anger and desire for revenge filled my mind; all the time I felt that if I ever came across that unknown enemy, I would tear him from limb to limb and extract my vengeance for this.

"After some days had passed in this manner, I gradually came to understand that this was my illusion and had no foundation in reality. Then, as the days went by I began to forget my grief and anger, both; but, I could not marry again. Ultimately, maybe my life would have gone by in this simplistic fashion, had not that man stepped into my shop at that inauspicious moment.

"I have heard that a drowning man clearly sees all the events of his past life flash like a picture on a screen before his eyes. Immediately on seeing this man, that is what happened to me. In a flash I recognized him-this was that heartless, who had killed my wife-daughter and father. Like a screen all those pictures flashed before my eyes. The helpless wailing of those passengers staring death in the face on that sinking ship began to resound in my ears. Once again I saw that sadistic smile of Vasco da Gama.

"The Judges had searched for the reason of my killing, they had asked questions, Babuji, what answer could I give! Even if I did who would have understood?

"Perhaps you will. I had seen it in your eyes and face. That is why I am putting you to this trouble. Though this will not have any effect, I know, but my heart will feel less burdened; besides that, I have no vested interest.

"I am ending here the history of this butcher's life that I have led. Now, Mirza Daud Bin Gholam Siddiqui is the name of one whose story I am beginning. Forget for the moment that I am this Mirza Daud. Imagine this to be someone else's life history.

"You will have heard of Calicut. Along the Malabar Coast, is this extremely beautiful jewel-like tiny city. Its boundaries extend to as far as the crowing of the bird goes. Behind the city are small hillocks, a valley, the Western Ghats—appearing to seclude this place from the rest of the world. Except for the overwhelming ocean there is no easy entry to or exit from Calicut. Along this ocean path innumerable merchant ships enter Calicut Port and then again, raising their sails fade away into the ocean. It is as if Calicut was the Mosaferkhana[6] for the shipping community of the entire world.

"The yellow-complexioned Chinese, the copper-hued Bengali, the golden-skinned Persian, the dark-skinned Moor-

---

6 **Mosaferkhana:** A resting place, a kind of tavern where a variety of people meet.

all move along the paths of Calicut with equal pride—none is inferior to the other. Lacquer and wood work from China, ivory from Burma, sandalwood from Malay, cotton silk bales, fine cotton, tiger skin from Bengal; special fans made of yaks' tail, musk and ornamental flower seeds from Champa and Magadh; fragrant wood, camphor, cinnamon from the south and pearls from Sri Lanka reach Calicut and are placed in heaps there. From the west, Turkish, Persian Arab and Moorish merchants buy them in exchange for gold and loading them on ships-some reach the mouth of the Euphrates through the Persian Sea and others anchor their ships near the Nile on the northern extremities of the Red Sea. From there all the merchandise of the Orient are scattered throughout the West. The king of Calicut, collecting taxes from the merchant ships, meets the expenses of the kingdom. The Royal treasury is always overflowing with gold and priceless jewels. There is no poverty in the kingdom anywhere, no discord or dissatisfaction; all sects of society are happy.

Mirza Daud is a respected merchant of Calicut. He has twenty-one merchant ships—their movements extend from Hwang Ho to the Nile. When this fleet of ships with their snow white sails upraised all set out on their ocean journey together, it seems as though a flock of swans are floating away on a blue sky.

Mirza Daud is a Moor. In Calicut, his palace of white marble is built according to Moorish tradition. His elderly father is still alive in far away Morocco; but he has accepted Calicut as his motherland. A number of foreign merchants have also done thus. Though a Muslim, Mirza Daud has only one wife. Recently, at the age of thirty-four a daughter was born to him. On his daughter's birthday Mirza Daud distributed a thousand tolas[7] of gold–then, a week long celebration took place at his house. The entire city praised him highly.

Truly there is no more popular or highly respected person than Mirza Daud in Calilcut. The high and the low, the rich and the poor–all respect him and look up to him. King Samari himself counts him as a friend. On the other hand—wealth continues to pour in thanks to business. Whatever brings happiness in this earth, he has no dearth of.

One summer evening, the sun is setting, colouring in scarlet the western horizon. As far as the eye can see the waters of the ocean, turning scarlet, are rippling along merrily. A gentle breeze has begun to blow, wafting along fragrance from faraway Lakshwadeep. There is not a trace of a cloud in the sky.

After coping with the heat all day, the men and women of the city have come crowding onto the jetty to savour the cool breeze. Extending for a long distance, the crescent-shaped jetty—structured in place by massive quadrangled boulders. There are rows of iron rings on the boulders to anchor the ships. During tides, water fills to the brim the area around the jetty and once again during ebb tide, leaving behind patches of wet, send it, retreating far back. This port is the heart of the city's commercial center. Buying and selling, bargaining, entertainment—everything takes place here. Hence, there is always a crowd.

At that time there was no newcomer, nor any outgoing merchant ships in the harbour. Work was somewhat slack.

---

7 **Tolas:** A measurement of weighing gold.

The citizens, dressed in a variety of strange clothes—some with wife and children, were strolling; there were others who were singing with full throated ease. Lively kids scampered about, playing, there were still others who plunged into the sea from the jetty, for a swim.

A Chinese magician was showing strange tricks. Sometimes loud peals of laughter were heard from the audience.

Catching hold of a somewhat plump Sinhalese, the magician peered into his ears and said, "There are two hundred and fifty pebbles in your head; if you permit, I can take them out." There were enthusiastic shouts from the crowds, "Take them out, take them out." The magician adroitly, with a minute pincer, began to extract pebbles, the size of betel nuts, and pile them on the ground. Waves of amusement broke out. Someone jestingly remarked, "Seth[8], I did not know that you were such a blockhead!"

Gradually the sun set colouring the ocean. The crimson light around that point on the horizon where the sun had set, gradually began to shrink. All of a sudden, on the breast of the ocean, in front of the scarlet hue, there were three dark shadows. All observed three ships entering the port.

Arguments broke out amongst the audience as to where the ships were coming from and to whom they belonged. Some said that they were Arabian and others that they were Chinese. But, as darkness descended, it could not definitely be deciphered which country the ships belonged to.

Mirza Daud was present at the port. For a long time he stared at the three ships. Gradually a shadow of concern

---

8 **Seth:** A rich and respected man of society.

overcast his face. In indistinct tones he said, "Portuguese ships! Where did these Phiringis surface from?"

No sooner had daylight faded on the horizon, than three vessels battered by the ocean lowered their tattered sails and entered the port of Calicut.

The next morning, as soon as dawn broke Mirza Daud presented himself at the port. He saw that quite a large crowd had gathered around some foreigners. They were speaking in some unknown tongue that none could understand; they were being asked questions in a variety of regional languages. Pushing the crowds aside, Mirza Daud came closer to them. Seeing him approach, everybody respectfully moved aside.

One of the newcomers asked, "Does nobody here know Portuguese? I want to speak to Zamorin and am looking for an interpreter."

Mirza Daud observed that the speaker was a man built like a tall and imposing tree; golden-complexioned, long golden hair and sharp features. The upper portion of his body was clad in a loose shirt, richly embroidered in gold and below he sported a loose tunic made of the same rich material, while the thighs to the feet were encased in a kind of armour made of leather. The feather in the cap he wore was positioned at an angle; the five-six other men who accompanied this man were all similarly clad. Swords hung at their waists.

Mirza Daud, minutely scrutinizing the appearance of this main protagonist, spoke gravely, "I understand Portuguese."

For a while the newcomer looked steadily at Mirza Daud's face. His face clouded. He spoke slowly, "I see that you are a Moor!"

The sharp disgust which lay buried in these words stung Mirza Daud. Not bothering to disguise his revulsion he answered, "Yes, I am a Moor. I see that you all are Portuguese pirates; this is not the first time that I am meeting the likes of you, but we are not on good terms with these Phiringis."

By now the second Portuguese spoke. He was young and spoke in arrogant tones, "We do not keep good terms with Moorish dogs—our religion is to oust them."

In an instant Mirza Daud's knife was unsheathed from his waist; his eyes blazed; the next moment, the leader of the newcomers, gesturing with his raised hands disarmed him. In humble tones he said, "Sir, forgive this arrogant companion of mine. It is true that you are Moorish and we are Portuguese; but we are both merchants and not pirates. No matter what happens elsewhere, here there is no discord between you and me. Rather, we will be obliged if we get your cooperation." Then, turning to his companion he said, "Pedro, if I ever hear such talk from you again, I will have each bone in your body broken under wheels and then fed to the dogs."

Pedro's face turned yellow with fright. In a voice that trembled inspite of the attempted bravado he asserted, "I am not afraid of speaking the truth. Why, you too said of the Moor...."

Before he had finished like lightening the hands of the first man clamped down on his throat. He pressed down on his windpipe for a while. When he let go, Pedro fell senseless to the ground. Not casting him another glance, the first man turned to Mirza Daud and said with a slight smile, "It is the duty of the religious to punish the liar. Now, if you kindly accompany me to the Zamorin and explain my appeal to him,

I will be extremely grateful to you," saying which he opened his hat and almost touching the ground extended his greetings. The audience who did not understand Portuguese, stared in amazement at this incomprehensible drama.

Mirza Daud was not taken in by the sweet tongue of the stranger and continued to maintain an obdurate silence. Ultimately, in a steady voice he said, "Phiringi, you are extremely crafty. Speak the truth as to why you have entered Samorin's kingdom."

"To trade."

"Christian, I know you all. Discord is your profession, greed is your religion and envy is your nature. There is no fighting or hatred in this kingdom—Hindus, Buddhists, Muslims, Hebrews–all carry on their trade and business in undisputed peace. Tell me the truth, why have you entered this kingdom?"

The Phiringi's face turned bloodless. Only his eyes like burning coal shone with an ineffective rage and envy; but, at the next moment, controlling himself and picking up the gold cross around his neck he offered, "I am swearing the truth on this cross, that except for trading by maintaining a good relationship with everybody, we have no ulterior motive."

Silently keeping his eyes fixed on his face Mirza Daud said, "I believe you. Come, let me take you all to Samari's palace."

Then, following Mirza Daud all the foreigners set off in the direction of the palace. Pedro's senseless body remained as though dead on the jetty.

Reaching the palace, kneeling before Samari, and kissing a corner of his garment, the leader of the Portuguese merchants said, "My name is Vasco da Gama nd I am the royal Emissary from Portugal. I request permission from you to carry on trading in Calicut." After this he gestured to his companions to lay before Samari the precious and expensive gifts sent by the king of Portugal.

No matter what had been said, Mirza Daud could not rid his mind of suspicion and disbelief. He knew Phiringis from a prior acquaintance-knew them being a Moor himself. In his own birth country, innumerable battles had further strengthened this acquaintance. They knew that the Phiringi was excessively greedy as regards money; and even more fond of leading a sybaritic existence. Their motherland did not yield wealth and hence to sustain themselves they had to physically labour hard and also mentally struggle through their lives. It was for this very reason that they envied the relatively prosperous Muslim community. To see another prosper was the bane of their existence. If they once got wind of wealth and prosperity anywhere, their greed and hunger would become so intense that by some means they would reach that place and establish themselves there. They would then flaunt their might, arrogance and persecution on friend and foe alike. They were very fond of fights, quarrels and were extremely adroit warriors. There was nothing that they could not do to preserve their own interests and to further the interests of their own nationality, would not hesitate even a little to sacrifice their own lives.

So far none had dared to come to India from Portugal by sea traversing through Africa; this path had not been known so far. Throwing open that path for the Europeans, Vasco da Gama had created innumerable possibilities and also causes for worry. Presently, Vasco da Gama's motives could not be clearly understood. However, the fact that he had stifled some underlying objective by throttling the arrogant and foul-mouthed Pedro did not escape the notice of Mirza Daud. Clouds of foreboding and doubts continued to overcast his mind.

The Portuguese began living in Calicut and each day began to fill their ships with merchandise. They purchased extremely inferior quality goods at twice and four times the value. No matter how euphoric that made the simple-minded traders feel, clouds of suspicion grew and intensified in the mind of a far-seeing merchant prince like Mirza Daud. It is not the norm for a merchant to buy goods at an enhanced price as compared to their actual worth, and the newcomers were neither inexperienced in business nor were they foolish. In which case the business was a mere pretext, some horrific goal lay submerged in guise. There was no end to the worry and concern the merchants felt.

Some time passed in this manner and the peaceful life in Calicut continued as before.

One spring, in the early morning, with white sails flying two ships entered the port. Immediately, news spread like wildfire in the city that Prabhakar Seth's ships were coming in from Bengal.

Prabhakar Seth was a renowned merchant. Every year at about this time his ships would arrive in Calicut, carrying textiles and other merchandise worth more than a lakh rupees. There would be a mad rush amongst the mercantile community of Calicut to buy shawls from Kashmir, special silks from Benaras and fine cotton bales from Bengal. Few brought such beautiful and valuable material, which is why Prabhakar enjoyed such renown.

Even before Prabhakar's vessel had touched the port, all the established merchants of the city had gathered there. From the ship itself Prabhakar began greeting all the people he knew. He had a way with words and was extremely fond of mysteries—and hence was a much loved figure.

The Hebrew, Musa Ibrahim, called him and said, "Prabhakar, seeing that it was getting late, this time we assumed that you would not be coming—crocodiles of your Sunderbans[9] had swallowed you for a meal."

"Musa Sahib, even if they had swallowed me, digesting me would have been impossible. Ah, Mirza sahib! Adab, adab![10] You are keeping well and everything else? This time I have got everything you ordered—lets see how much you can take. I see that the sword at your waist is new—from Damascus, is it? There is no way but I have to have a pair— have given my word to the King of Gour. That reminds me, at Srikhanda I met your ship going towards Java—all is well. There is Hyder Mustafa! How many times have you married so far? You will be committing a great sin if you do not have Spanish grape this time. Jumbo, do not bare all your teeth laughing—hold the anchor."

After the boat had been anchored, Prabhakar embraced and greeted everybody. Then, Mirza Daud asked, "Prabhakar, what merchandise have you brought?"

---

9 **Sunderbans:** Largest mangrove swamp in the world.
10 **Adab:** A form of greeting usually used by muslims.

Prabhakar answered, "You have not seen such fine cotton like the one I have got this time. It is softer than a spider's web and lighter than thistledown—a hundred and fifty yards of material can be grasped in one fist full. But, one bale of cloth is worth five tolas of gold—cannot afford to give it for less. They had wanted to give up to four tolas in Cochin, but I did not accept. Could I return home with a loss? The Sethni[11] would not even have looked at me."

Mirza Daud laughed. "Let her not look then! It will be of no loss to the Sethni not to look at you. Now, show me your wares."

Prabhakar said, "What are you talking about, Mirza sahib? It won't be a loss? The Sethni is a young woman—presumably she is at the prime of her youth; now if she cannot look at her husband, her entire life and youth will be a loss! That reminds me, the last time I had heard that your wife was not keeping well. Is there any good news?"

Mirza Daud replied, "With Khoda's grace, a daughter has been born."

Prabhakar said, "You had kept quiet about this very good news all this while? In our country it is believed that a daughter's birth increases the life span of a father. Then, tonight there is an invitation for me at your home. In my country, feasting on chicken is a problem–neither are they very common; and the Brahmins cause a lot of problems. Oh God! Who are these people, Mirza Sahib? I have never seen such a mode of dressing in my life. Where did they spring from?"

---

11 **Sethni**: Wife of the Seth.

Mirza Daud turned around and found Vasco da Gama and two of his companions heading in that direction. In the meanwhile both had run into each other on the streets of Calicut, but none had evinced any desire to get better acquainted with the other. Rather, they had avoided each other as far as possible.

Responding to Prabhakar's question, Mirza Daud said, "They are Portuguese. Gradually you will get to know them."

In the meanwhile, the goods from Prabhakar's ship was being unloaded on to the jetty for all to examine. All the merchants had crowded around to watch. Mirza Daud too joined them. Vasco da Gama also came along from another direction.

Seeing the quality of the textile Mirza Daud said, "Very superior quality textile. Prabhakar, how much of this have you brought?"

Proudly Prabhakar answered, "One whole shipload."

Daud said, "Very well, I am taking the entire ship. The price etc. will be fixed tonight."

Vasco da Gama never before had seen such exquisite fine cotton fabric. Truly, such fine cotton bales were not sent anywhere except Persia. What went to Portugal, Spain, France and other western countries was of a relatively inferior quality. Da Gama's covetous spirits were aroused. To draw attention of the Pope and King Emmanuel, what better gift could there be? He said, "I will buy the cotton."

Smiling, Mirza Daud said, "There is no way of doing that. I have bought the fabric."

Turning to Prabhakar, Da Gama said, "I will pay a higher price."

Mirza Daud said, "You cannot get it even by paying a greater price–this textile is now mine."

Turning a deaf ear is him and addressing Prabhakar, Da Gama said, "I will pay double the price."

Irritated, Mirza Daud said, "Even if you pay a hundred times more, it will not be yours."

With the speed of lightening Da Gama turned towards Mirza Daud. In harsh tones, he said, "Moor, be silent – I am talking to the owner of the merchandise."

Prabhakar was intelligent. Mirza Daud was an old customer, while he did not even know this person. He said, "Da-Gama, I had already realized it, but today your true nature has come to light. Trading is a mere pretext, you are a marauder. Why else would you want to spoil commerce by this unfair price?"

Like a wounded tiger Vasco da Gama pulled out the sword from his scabbard. Grinding his teeth and enraged, he said, "Moor, today with your blood I will wash away the disgrace of this sword."

Mirza Daud too unsheathed his sword and cried out, 'Heathen Phiringi, today I will send you to hell!'

Within minutes the anxious crowds had moved back, making a large circle for the Ju-Jutsus[12] to fight it out. Though a peaceful trading center, such scenarios were not absolutely unknown in Calicut. It was not unknown to anybody that a dispute which had reached the stage of a final decision by the sword was not only useless to try and dissipate, but also extremely dangerous. Everybody moved aside and allowed

---

12 **Ju-Jutsu:** Aparticular formof the martial arts.

each party to find a solution to the controversy through the medium of weapons.

The poisonous glances that had been exchanged when Vasco da Gama and Mirza Daud had first looked at each other had continued to gather in the heart of both–till, finding a very simple pretext, it had flared up into this irreversible enmity. Both realised that this enmity could only come to an end with the death of either one.

The two sword holders stood at the center of the circle of silent spectators. Vasco da Gama was massive, hard as a rock and as strong as an elephant. Mirza Daud was relatively slightly built and short; but like a deadly poisonous snake extremely agile, forceful and full of life. Vasco da Gama's sword was a s supple as a whip, as sharp; Mirza Daud's sword was relatively curved and sharp. Both inspected each other with their unsheathed weapons for a while. Then, like a storm, with his sword pointing ahead, Vasco da Gama charged.

Before Da Gama's sword could touch Mirza Daud, with his own sword he adroitly deflected the move and stood aside; at the next instance his curved sword stabbed Da Gama's thigh and returned. Da Gama moved back and tried to defend himself, but could not. His thigh armour steadily became soaked with blood.

Da Gama did not pay any heed to that, but became very careful. He began to wield his sword in a more disciplined and wary manner. It would not do to treat his opponent with disdain. Mirza Daud was extraordinarily adept at wielding the sword, a second mistake would leave him no chance for rectification.

The Scarlet Dusk 23

On the other hand, Mirza Daud also realised that Da Gama was his equal in sword play and at the same time was also doubly stronger. True, he was neither as fast nor as light on his feet–but, his sword was supple and long, while his was curved and shorter. His mode of fighting too was completely different. In this respect, Mirza Daud observed that Da Gama was more likely to win. Mirza Daud began to battle very carefully.

Just as a snake and mongoose, while locked in combat stare unblinkingly and assess each other—and lose no opportunity of attacking at lightening speed and again retreating to their original position, Da Gama and Mirza Daud too began to wage a similar battle. Weapon struck against weapon and jangled noisily every minute, sunlight danced off the glistening swords in sparks, like lightening. The still human circle watched this strange battle with rapt attention.

While fighting Mirza Daud began constantly jibing Da Gama with poisonous barbed remarks, "Phiringi marauder, look at your blood—not red like that of a human, but blue like that of the devil! Christian dog! Even now beg for forgiveness and I will spare your life."

Without answering, Da Gama battled on silently. It was clear to the cunning Da Gama that by jibing at him, Mirza Daud was trying to make him lose his cool. The battle gradually grew more intense and fierce. Both warriors were breathing deeply and their entire bodies were dripping sweat; but, both seemed to be encased in an invisible armour. Da Gama's sword repeatedly returned futilely from Mirza Daud's throat, his chest; Mirza Daud's sword buzzed around Da Gama like a swarm of angry bees, unable to sting.

Suddenly Da Gama noticed with fright that, moving around, he had reached the absolute edge of the jetty and another step would drop him straight into the waters of the ocean. Looking at the expression on his face, Mirza Daud laughed aloud. In a voce dripping with sardonic venom he said, "Phiringi, today I will soak you in the waters of the ocean. Then, like a dead rat, will send you to your King Emannuel as a gift."

At long last, what Mirza Daud had been aiming for all this while happened—Da Gama lost his patience. With a roar like that of a mad wild boar, holding aloft his sword, he charged towards Mirza Daud. If he had so wanted, Mirza Daud could easily have killed Da Gama; but instead of doing that, with the reverse side of his sword, he struck Da Gama on his left fist. Immediately the sword flew out of his hand and moving through space, fell some distance away.

Da Gama's two companions had so far been watching the duel along with all the others. Seeing their master's sudden and unexpected downfall, they moved forward to help him. But, no sooner had they taken two steps, when the gigantic jet black Jumbo, extending his mast-like hands and grasping them by the tuft of their hair, brought them back; though they did not understand what he said with a full display of glittering white teeth, it was not difficult at all for them to comprehend Jumbo's heartfelt desire.

Holding his sword at Da Gama's throat, Mirza Daud said, "Da Gama, kneel, or else I will kill you."

Da Gama did not kneel. Baring his breast and with a distorted smile he said, "Moor, of course it is your nature to kill the unarmed."

Thinking for a while Mirza Daud replied, "Fine, I will let you go, but promise........."

Da Gama answered, "I will not make any promise, do what you will."

Mirza Daud said, "Promise that within seven days you will leave this country along with all your companions and never return."

Da Gama laughed aloud and said, "Moor, you are an utter fool! I will not make any promise. Kill me. If my blood stains the soil of Calicut, it will be easy for Emmanuel to establish his flag of victory in Hind[13]."

Mirza Daud smiled and said, "After all these days, at least you have yourself revealed what your actual intentions are. But I will not let you be successful. Emannuel's Flag of Victory will not be established in Calicut. It will always remain the place where all races of the world mingle. Promise or else..."

Da Gama frowned and asked, "Or else?"

"Or else I will not let even one person remain alive to return to Portugal. Your ship will be burnt and these one hundred and thirty people I will throw into the sea after cutting them into little pieces."

There was a stunned silence from Da Gama. He did not answer.

Mirza Daud once again said, "Da Gama, even now promise—I will trust your religion and let you go. Think of the fact that if you die, who will direct all your beggar countrymen here?"

---

13 **Hind**: India.

In a muffled voice Da Gama said, "I promise..."

Mirza Daud said, "Promise on Mother Mary of your Jesus."

In a voice trembling with rage Da Gama promised that he would leave the country within a week and never again step on the soil of Bharat.[14]

Freeing Da Gama, Mirza Daud and some other eminent citizens of the city met Samari. After listening to a detailed description of the entire proceedings Samari said, "As long as they do not openly cause any damage to my kingdom. But, if any of you have been caused any personal harm, you can take revenge and I will not stop you."

Everybody tried to convince Samari that they were extremely cunning and skilful in war, they possessed cannons, guns and ammunition; if they got an opportunity, they would usurp the golden and heavenly kingdom by force.

Smiling, Samari answered, "It is true that I do not have armed forces, but this Samari dynasty since the 15th century has been ruling the kingdom in this region—nobody has been able to oust them. My throne is established on popularity and a healthy reign. What can they do to me?"

All returned disappointed.

A week later, bearing the truce framed by Samari on a golden scroll, Vasco da Gama and his companions boarded the ship.

Mirza Daud called out from the port and said, "Da Gama, remember your oath."

A cunning smirk played across Da Gama's face; keeping his gaze steadily fixed on Mirza Daud he said, "Mirza Daud, we will meet again."

---

14 **Bharat**: India.

Mirza Daud smiled and answered, "That is impossible. I am a Muslim and will go to Behest[15]."

Shooting burning embers of anger from his eyes Da Gama said, "We will meet again in this life time itself."

Then, steadily his three ships left the port.

Four years went by. Though what happened in these four years is not relevant to the story, a brief description is given. Two years after Vasco da Gama left Calicut, Portuguese ships came to India once again. This time the leader of the Portuguese was a priest by name of Alvarez Coblar and under him were nine ships. Immediately on entering the port of Calicut, the priest Alvarez started assaulting the city with cannons from the ship. A lot of citizens died, many more were injured and quite a few palaces were razed. In this manner, after instilling fear and a sense of duty in the minds of the king and citizens alike, the Portuguese once again entered India. King Samarin honoured the newcomers and gave permission for them to construct their habitation on land granted to them on the outskirts of the city boundaries. But, due to this unreasoning, vengeful manner and cruelty, a feeling of disgust and distaste began to grow towards them in the minds of the general public of Calicut.

Then, it did not take much time for disputes to begin. Those who were left with a personal animosity towards the arrogant foreigners, picked fights resulting in bloodshed. The Portuguese also responded in kind. Gradually the fire of discord began to spread inside and outside. One day the citizens set fire to the dwellings of the Portuguese and killed

---

15 **Behest:** Heaven, as according to the Muslim faith.

seventy of the Phiringis. The remaining escaped to the ship and from there set alight a section of the city by firing cannons. Then they left Calicut, not returning for another two years.

The King and the citizens of Calicut breathed a sigh of relief thinking that the nuisance had gone and would not reappear.

About an year after the aforementioned incident, Mirza Daud with his wife and child went to his motherland Morocco. After staying there for a while, taking his aged father along, they paid a visit to Mecca-Sharif[16]. After their pilgrimage they were on the way to returning to Calicut.

Mirza Daud was supposed to return to Calicut from Mecca while his father would go back to Morocco. But the latter was getting on in years and did not have very long to live. Maybe there would be no opportunity to visit Morocco again in the near future, his father might not live that long a time; thinking of all this, Mirza Daud did not allow him to return, but brought him back to Calicut along with himself. The man, looking on his tiny grand-daughter, as beautiful as the full moon of Id[17] had forgotten all else and did not raise too many objections.

While visiting Mecca, Mirza Daud had run into some eminent citizens of Calicut. He told them, "You are also returning to Calicut. Join us in my ship." Gladly, along with their families, they joined Mirza Daud in his ship.

---

16 **Mecca-Sharif:** The holiest religious shrine of the Muslims.
17 **Id:** Religious celebration of the Muslim community, centred on a particular constellation of the moon.

It was a three month journey from Mecca to Calicut. At the scheduled time the ship moved away from the coastline and crossed the Red Sea. Gradually they moved over the Persian Sea and entered the Indian Ocean.

On the mighty ocean, the wind fanning out the sails, Mirza Daud's ship began to move in a southern direction. All around; the bottomless waters shimmered and swelled—like a million bits of shattered mirror the sun was reflected therein. The horizon like an unbroken margin encircled the ship all around. Only in the very distant horizon, like a mass of clouds in the east, a glimpse of the verdant greenery of the Kutch region could be seen.

The experienced pilot of the ship said that if the speed and direction of the wind did not change, by eight they would reach Calicut. Thinking of the imminent end of the journey all were happy.

The day Friday–the sun gradually moved from its overhead position and progressively started sinking in the western horizon. On the sprawling roof of the ship Mirza Daud, his father and the other male members present had almost finished the second Namaaz[18] of the day. The controller of the ship, staring steadily ahead stood still and unmoving in front of the helm. Everything was silent all around except for the tumultuous waves set into motion by the ship—and the foam, which seemed to laugh in merriment.

All of a sudden, shattering the silence of the skies and the atmosphere all around, there was a noise like the terrifying thundering of clouds. Everybody was astounded to observe

---

18 **Namaaz:** Prayers offered by the Muslim.

five Phiringi ships, raising all sails and simultaneously making use of innumerable oars—like a many-legged gigantic sea beast rushing towards them. Unobserved, they had come so close that even the men on the ships were clearly visible. At this unexpected sight, bewildered, everybody stared unblinkingly in that direction.

It was indeed an astonishing spectacle! Only moments before there had not been even a small boat in sight. From what unknown cave in the depths of the ocean did these terrible monsters spring from? Mirza Daud's heart said that that was the end. They had announced their presence by firing cannons—today no mercy would be shown. That was when desire for avenging themselves with the Moor's blood would be fulfilled.

An incident of this sort had never before been seen on the breast of the ocean. Since time immemorial, innumerable ships and boats had sailed, unobstructed along these ways. From China to the Caspean Sea, there had never been sea pirates or the like. Since the waterways were relatively safer as compared to the land routes, maritime trading had become widespread. But today, the easy passage of goods which had been in existence through the ages was blocked by cannon-wielding Phiringis, blindly pursuing their self-interest.

However, it was impossible for Mirza Daud to engage in war. His ship was a ship of pilgrims and carried no weapons or firearms. It only consisted of some helpless pilgrims inexperienced in warfare and some even more helpless women and children. In these circumstances it would only be insanity to battle against five war ships. The only option was to flee;

but Mirza Daud's ship had sails, their adversary possessed sails and oars both; in such a case even escape was impossible.

Mirza Daud silently thought for a while. He once looked up at the sky. The sky was almost cloudless—it was all but evening. There was still some time before nightfall. He called all the men and told them to raise every single sail and ensure that the ship move as fast as possible.

But no sooner had this order been given than cannons were fired from all five ships together. One cannon rent the largest sail, moved across the ship and fell into the ocean on the other side, the others all fell into the water around. None however could cause serious damage to the ship.

The men aboard the ship grew pale. From below, the wailing and pitiful pleas of frightened children and women could be heard. Clenching his teeth, Mirza Daud commanded the sailors, "Sail the ship as long as you can—we will not surrender to the Phiringi pirates."

In the meanwhile Mirza Daud's four-year old daughter panted up to her father and embraced his thigh. She said, "Father, Mother is calling you," and looking up at her father started crying loudly "Father, I am very scared."

Picking up his daughter, Mirza Daud pressed her close to his chest. He whispered in her ears, "Haruna, do not weep. You are the daughter of a Moor—what are you scared of? Today we will all journey to Behest together."

Handing over his daughter to his father Mirza Daud went down. Right in front he saw his distraught wife.

Taking out a miniature bejeweled knife from his waist and handing it to his wife, in calm and measured tones he said, "Saleha, probably the time has come to breathe our last. Pirate ships are chasing us. If they step onto this ship, use this knife on yourself. Do not do anything before that. Assure the other women, tell them not to be afraid without cause. I am leaving." Saying this Mirza Daud clasped his wife's head to his breast for a moment and returned upstairs.

He saw that in the interim period, the pirate ships had surrounded them in a semi-circle. They had come so close that even their voices could be clearly heard. Mirza Daud saw that from each ship all cannons were aimed in their direction. There could be no miss from such close quarters.

Mirza Daud's father came up and said, "Daud, there is no way out. Unless we surrender, all of us have to drown."

Mirza Daud answered, "Even if we surrender, we will have to die; it is better to die by drowning."

His father replied, "That is true. But there are children and women with us. Shouldn't we try to protect them?"

Thinking for a while Mirza Daud said, "But, will the marauders take pity on women and children? Rather..."

His father said, "The Phiringis are greedy for money, in exchange for money they might set us free."

The other men too spoke in support of the old man. Mirza Daud then said, "Fine, let us try."

At that moment a cannon was fired from a ship. The massive mast along with the sails came crashing down and immediately the piled-up sails, made of cloth, caught fire.

The women so far had maintained their decorum by remaining inside the hold of the ship, but now they forgot all sense of any shame. Mothers with children in their arms and the childless, in whatever condition they were, came up, wailing and scared out of their wits. Kneeling down, some sent up fervent prayers to God to spare their lives, others, holding their babies high above their heads with both hands, tried to evoke the compassion of the pirates.

The fire from the sails gradually began to spread throughout the ship. Gathering water from the ocean the men tried to douse the flames. After much difficulty the flames were quenched. For the moment the ship won a respite.

A Phiringi vessel had come right up to Mirza Daud's ship—the distance was only about a hundred yards or so. Turning the guns around they were about to fire another round of cannons, when Mirza Daud called out to them, "Do not fire, we are surrendering."

Leaving the cannons, the pirates began rejoicing. One of them, probably the captain called out, "Throw all the weapons you have into the water or else we will fire."

Mirza Daud said, "We have no arms with us. This is a ship of pilgrims. All the wealth we have will be handed to you—let us go."

Conversation of this sort was going on, when a man from the attacking ship came up. An extremely richly attired, massive figure of a man. Seeing him Mirza Daud's blood suddenly ran cold. He recognised who it was—Vasco da Gama.

Like a jet black poisonous snake, malignity lay coiled on his face. Looking at Mirza Daud, Vasco da Gama laughed. Taking off his feathered cap and sweeping it to the ground, he said, "Mirza Daud, a good morning to you today. Had I not said that we would meet again?"

All of a sudden Mirza Daud found no words to speak. Then, turning to the captain, Vaco Da Gama in harsh tones said, "Captain, why are the cannons silent? Have you forgotten my command?"

The frightened captain answered, "My Lord, in exchange of their wealth they are asking for freedom."

The two ships gradually drew closer. Once again turning towards Mirza Daud, in sharp barbed tones Vasco Da Gama asked, "Moor, you are begging for freedom in exchange for your wealth?"

Mirza Daud said, "I do not beg for my own life. Take everything that we have, but set free the old, the women and the children."

Da Gama slowly savoured the sweet flavour of his enemy's humiliation and said, "Set free the old, the women and the children? But, what do we stand to gain by that? Rather, if you send across your young women to us, the lives of your men might be saved. There is a need for women in our ship. Not for me–for my *khalasis*[19]. I do not have a taste for women."

Mirza Daud's face turned colourless in rage and insult. He realized that Da Gama was playing with him. Controlling himself with great difficulty he responded,. "Da Gama, it disgusts me to answer your proposal. If you so desire you can take all the valuable goods and gold and silver that is with us and give us freedom. Or you will get nothing at all."

Da Gama frowned and asked, "Will get nothing at all—what do you mean?"

Mirza Daud said, "That means, by force you can kill us, but will not be able to achieve much else. If you forcibly try

---

19 **Khalasis**: menial belonging to the slup.

to board the ship, I will have the planks removed and sink the ship."

The frown on Da Gama's face deepened and, lowering his face he began to think.

On the other hand, due to the mast crumbling, Mirza Daud was as helpless to move as an elephant stuck in a more of mud. The five Phiringi ships closed in on him from all three directions.

Impatiently Mirza Daud called out, "Da Gama, whatever you decide, do so soon. We have twelve hundred tolas of gold with us and some other articles of great value; if you want them, let us know fast; should you delay too much, you stand to lose everything."

Da Gama asked, "You will not give us your women?"

Mirza Daud thundered aloud, "No, we will not. We do not trade in wives and children."

Da Gama said, "Moor, your audacity has not lessened a jot! Fine, I will accept your wealth. Whatever is in your ship, send it across in a raft."

"If whatever is there is sent, will you release us?"

"I will."

"How can one trust you?"

"I do not lie."

"Liar, you had promised not to step onto Hind again, what about that?"

Da Gama laughed and said, "I have still not stepped onto Hind."

Mirza Daud then consulted with all the others. Everyone said, "Since we have been caught in their tentacles, there is no way out but to believe them." Left with no choice, Mirza Daud agreed.

Then, preparing a raft and loading it with whatever was there, even the jewellery worn by the women, everything was sent to Da Gama's ship.

Da Gama asked, "Don't you have anything more?"

"No."

"Am asking once again—won't you give your women?"

In unbearable rage Mirza Daud could not speak. Only his eyes began to burn like flames.

Vasco da Gama smiled a poisonous smile. He said, "Fire, as you will." Then, turning back to the captain he said, "Captain, bombard their ship with cannons and set it on fire. Today we will burn to death those Muslim dogs."

Mirza Daud shrieked aloud, "Cheat! Traitor! Lying Devil!"

Da Gama said, "Mirza Daud, the world does not contain so much wealth that will grant you your life. But you can still save your life in exchange of your wife. I will keep her as a slave."

Mirza Daud shouted like one gone mad, "Devil! Devil!"

There was a great furore in the ship. Men and women began rushing about madly in all directions. Everybody appeared to be trying to escape that accursed ship. From all directions heart-rending pleas arose, "Protect us! Be merciful! Save us!"

An answer came to this fervent prayer. Suddenly like a hailstorm bullets were showered on the ship. Some died and others were wounded. The nightmare of death began to assume a dreadful form.

Mirza Daud's father, clutching little Haruna to his breast, trembling, came and stood beside his son. In choked tones he called out only once, "Daud!"

Racked with emotions, Mirza Daud embraced his father and daughter; at this time, forgetting all about decorum, Saleha came and stood beside her husband and held his hands.

Mirza Daud looked at them with misty eyes. In a voice choking with emotion he asked, "Father, is there no God?"

Suddenly with a little whimper, Haruna slumped back. Quickly picking up his daughter in his lap, Mirza Daud found that she had breathed her last. A cruel bullet had pierced her chest.

In rapid succession his wife and father were felled to the ground by bullets and lay writhing in the throes of a death agony. Then, Vasco da Gama, with a smoking gun in his hands smiled a satanic smile.

The sun was touching the western horizon. Both, the sky and the ocean, like simmering blood turned scarlet. It was sunset on the breast of the ocean.

Now, all five ships fired together. With the onslaught of bullets, like a very old man suffering in the cold, Mirza Daud's ship shook and trembled. Once again the sails caught fire. Gradually swaying, the ship began to sink. Once again the cannons fired. Now, the front of the ship was completely shattered. With a rippling sound, water began flowing in.

Then, within minutes all was over. A great wailing was heard of the combined voices of all those on board. Suddenly the burning ship stood upright, as though living; it then plunged rapidly into the depths of the ocean. The voices of the passengers crying out were stilled. Where moments before there had been a ship, innumerable waves played about in merriment.

As motionless as painted pictures, the Phiringi ships stood silent. In the twilight darkness they appeared like ghost ships belonging to some other world.

Very shortly after, shattering the silence of the evening, blaring war trumpets and horns were heard aboard Vasco da Gama's ship.

Incomparable

ONE

Owing to the insurmountable dictums of nature when domestic squabbles arose between Byomkesh and Satyabati, I would sit back impartially and relish them. But when this bickering centred around the relative superiority of the male species as versus the female, I was forced to side with Byomkesh. Even then, in spite of both friends joining forces, we were not always a match for Satyabati. Truly, there are so many recorded instances of the misdeeds of males in the history of mankind that to negate them is virtually impossible. Finally, we had to quit the arena.

For some time, a particular form of disturbance was becoming very much the norm in Kolkata: one winter morning, sitting with the newspapers to the accompaniment of cups of tea, that is what Byomkesh and I were discussing. The matter which was continuing to recur, proceeded roughly along these lines—one or more women, belonging to good families would set out in the afternoon. The men would all have left for work and the housewives would be finishing their meal and preparing for the afternoon siesta. At this time the girl would knock on the door. If the housewife was cautious and called out "Who is that?" from outside the answer would be, 'There are some embroidered blouses and petticoats[1] going very cheap. Are you interested?' The housewife, thinking that it was a saleswoman would open the door and immediately young women would enter and at gun point or knife point decamp with all the money and jewellery.

This sort of incident had happened a couple of times, but the perpetrators had not been apprehended. Opening the newspaper that day I found a similar incident had taken place in a household in Kashipur. I read out the news to Byomkesh. With a sardonic smile he said, "What's so surprising about this? Women always commit thefts in the afternoons."

At this moment Satyabati entered the room. Standing near the door and casting a mocking glance at Byomkesh she remarked, "Oh really! Girls commit dacoity in the afternoons and all of you remain saints!"

Byomkesh had not intended Satyabati to hear, but since she had not only heard, but also responded, he could not retreat. He said, "I did not say that we are all saints, but you all are no less."

Thus the argument began. Sitting on the edge of the bed Satyabati said, "It is in your very nature to criticize females. Just let me hear what women have done."

Byomkesh said, "Not much, just dacoity in broad daylight."

I read aloud the portion about the afternoon dacoity from the newspaper. Satyabati answered, "Accepted that this was wrong of them, they have made a mistake in choosing this

---

1 **Petticoat:** A long kind of skirt worn underneath the sari.

as a means of filling their stomachs. But, when you all go about murdering and wounding, causing wars to break out and thereby killing thousands—is that nothing? In comparison to you, how many murders have females committed?"

Seeing the situation getting out of hand, Byomkesh said, "Since you all were housebound all this while, it wasn't possible to do anything. Now, having gained independence, your bravado is increasing. Bankimchandra[2] had composed *Debi Chaudhurani*[3] such a long time ago. Even in those times and being a female, look at her! If she had been a modern girl, can you imagine what she might have done, Ajit?"

Shaking her head, Satyabati said, "You can't pull the wool over my eyes with all that rubbish. How many actual examples can you give where women have committed murders?"

Byomkesh answered, "You want examples! Why, just the other day, in the Zenana Phatak[4], a female prisoner killed the gaol guard and made good her escape."

Satyabati laughed aloud, "Two months ago a woman killed someone. Just give me an account of the number of murders you all have committed in these two months."

Even in today's papers there was a reference to a murder perpetrated by a man, but I glossed over that; instead I said, "There is an example in today's paper about the inhuman nature of women. A washer-man had snagged a woman's

---

2 **Bankimchandra:** One of the most renowned authors in Bengali literature.
3 **Debi Chaudhurai:** One of the compositions of Bankimchandra, centring around a dynamic lady, whom circumstances had turned into the queen of dacoity on the waterways.
4 **Zenana Phatak:** Womens' Doorway .

expensive sari; the lady with a large kitchen knife sliced off his nose. The man in a serious condition has been hospitalized and it is doubtful whether he would survive."

Satyabati smiled, "There is also none to rival you all at lying. You people are lying thieves, dacoits, murderers......"

I do not know how far this argument would have gone, but at this moment there was a knock on the outer door. With the demeanour of a victor, her head held high, Satyabati went inside. Opening the door I found that it was the postman; handing over a long and thick envelope he left.

It was addressed to Byomkesh, but there was no reference to the sender. I handed it to him; doubtfully examining it he said, "Seems to be the manuscript of a budding author. Send it to Prabhat."

Ever since we had entered the world of book publishing, prospective new authors frequently sent us their manuscripts in all enthusiasm; so, a thick envelope had the effect of making Byomkesh rather tense.

I said, "It might not be a manuscript. Why don't you open it and take a look?"

He responded, "Why don't you do so?"

I did. True, it was not a manuscript. But, someone had sent Byomkesh a lengthy letter, almost equaling a short story. Greatly relieved, Byomkesh stretched out on the couch and said, "It can't be a love letter. So, you read it aloud and let me listen."

Drawing up a couch beside the chair I began to read the letter. The handwriting was not very clear, and it took a bit of effort to read; but the Bengali was very smooth flowing.—

Sri Byomkesh Baskshi,

Incomparable 43

Respectful Greetings,

My name is Sri Chintamani Kundu. The police are trying to implicate me in a murder case, hence, left with no other choice, I am seeking your help. If I had the strength I would have personally called on you, hearing about it directly from me would have clarified matters much more. But since the last couple of years I have been immobile due to an attack of paralysis. My left side cannot be used; I can only move about in my room a little. Hence I am forced to write to you.

After describing the grave matter which has taken place, I would like to introduce myself. My age now is fifty seven years; there is no wife-child, just three houses. The road is fairly broad; the house in which I live is on one side of the road, my other two houses are facing it—almost directly opposite, on the other side of the road. These houses are relatively small and one-storied; one can call them twin houses. There is a narrow alley; between the two houses, going towards the rear portion.

Seeing my address on the letter-head you will have made out that I live in the east-south section of the city.

I am crippled with sickness and these two rooms constitute my whole world. Before being struck by paralysis, I was an agent; running about was what I was used to. So, now the entire day I spend sitting in front of the window, watching people go by. With the help of a pair of binoculars I have bought, I look at distant objects. Thanks to them, the interior of a lot of houses can also be observed. I can keep an eye on the tenants of my twin houses. Those who are able, go for movies and to the theatre; sitting in front of the window, with my naked eyes I watch life flow by and with the help of the binoculars take note of the background. You will be amazed to hear of the sheer variety of scenes that I have seen. But, let that be.

About one and a half months ago, towards the middle of the month of Pous[5], a young man came to meet me. He was short and squat, with brownish hair, a mobile face and a butterfly moustache just below his nose. He supported expensive western clothes, and on top, an overcoat made of camel-hair material. From the doorway he respectfully said, 'My name is Tapan Sen, may I come in?'

At the time I was sitting by the window reading the newspaper; looking up I said, 'Come in.'

Tapan Sen pulled up a chair and sat in front of me. I asked, 'Tell me, what can I do for you?'

Pointing outside the window he said, 'One of your twin houses has fallen vacant. That's why I am here, if you will rent it to me.'

The house had been lying vacant for a while, I had had it repaired and painted; but I had made up my mind that unless I got a good tenant, I would not rent it out. He seemed to be pleasant enough on first acquaintance. I asked, 'How do you earn a living?'

He took out a cigarette tin from the overcoat pocket, but then put it away; probably in deference to my advanced years he did not light up. Tapan Sen said, 'I work in a newspaper office, Night Editor. I work through the night and sleep through the day,' saying which he smiled.

---

5 **Pous:** About the middle of December.

I asked, 'Who else is there in your family?'

Gently he responded, 'I have just set up a family—my wife and I. There is nobody else.'

In my heart of hearts I was pleased. Children tend to spoil the house, drawing with ink on the walls. I said, 'Fine, I will rent to you—that will be rupees one hundred fifty.'

Hesitantly he said, 'That is a bit steep for me.'

I said, 'It is a furnished house–beds, tables, chairs and cupboards–you will find everything.'

'That's fine then. Will it be possible to take a look at the house?'

I handed him the key and Tapan went and saw the house. Then, handing me one hundred and fifty rupees, he said, 'Here is a month's rent.'

Writing out a receipt for him I asked, 'When do you plan to shift?'

He said, 'Tomorrow is the first of the month according to the English calendar. The house is lying empty, if you permit, I can shift in sometime today itself.'

I said, 'Fine, come whenever it is convenient.'

Tapan Sen left with the key. Assuming that I had got a good tenant, I felt very pleased with myself.

That day I spent the entire evening by the window, looking towards the house; but Tapan did not turn up along with his wife.

In the morning, opening the windows, I found that they had come. They must have turned up sometime at night with their luggage.

My curious eyes strayed in that very direction. At about nine thirty, a young girl closed the front door from inside. A few moments later she left, through the door at the rear.

Then I had a good look at her. She was tall and slim and had a good length of hair coiled loosely at the nape of her neck, a small attaché was in her hands. I assumed that Tapan was sleeping after the nights work and so his wife had gone shopping.

The whole afternoon went by, but she did not return. Finally, she returned around four thirty in the evening. Not ringing the front door bell, she went by the alley to the rear. Probably she did not want to wake up her husband.

A while later, I sent Ramdhin over. They were new tenants and I should enquire whether they were facing any problems etc. Through the window I saw Ramdhin going up and knocking at the door. The girl opened the door. After talking to Ramdhin, the girl once raised her eyes and looked up at my window; then she accompanied Ramdhin to meet me.

I had seen her from a distance, now I saw her at close quarters. Very good-looking and slim–there was no excess fat anywhere; on her left cheek was a reddish mole, which only enhanced the beauty of her face. One point I noted, husband and wife were almost of the same age–about twenty-three/twenty-four. Maybe they had fallen in love and married. These days a lot of that can be seen. Respectfully greeting me she said, 'My name is Shanta. There are no problems at all; we have found a lovely house.' Her manner of talking was as sweet as her tones were gentle.

I said, 'Sit down, you.......'

She shook her head, 'No, you must not address me so formally, I am your daughter's age.'

Agreeing, I replied, 'All right. If you need servants, this is a new locality........'

She said, 'No need for servants. We are only a family of two. I can handle all the work.'

I answered, 'Fine, fine. So, you had gone out in the morning and are returning now. Where were you all day?'

She replied, 'I teach in a school. There's a small school in Chetla–am a teacher there. Let me take my leave now, will have to prepare his food. He will be leaving for work in the evening.' Smiling a bit, Shanta nodded and left.

I liked both of them. Presently, tenants constitute my entire life. They live in my house, pay rent and are involved in their own work; there's no interaction. The other section of the twin houses is occupied by a Madrasi family; they do not understand my language, at the end of the month they pay the rent and collect the receipt. There is no bonding with them. But, this young Bengali couple had captured my heart.

Sitting by the window I saw Tapan, in a coat and pants leaving by the rear alley; he lit a cigarette, standing before the street lamp in front of our house and then moved away along the bus route. He would remain away all night, returning towards dawn, after finishing work.

Thereafter their routine work continued. In the morning, around nine thirty, Shanta would leave for school and return in the evening. Tapan leaves in the evening and I do not know when he returns. Their lives are very tranquil; no visitors come in to the house, perhaps they do not know many people close by. After Tapan leaves at night, the electric lights in the house are switched off, only a mild candle burns in the front room. That too is extinguished by eight. Shanta probably goes to bed early after a hard day's work.

I remain very curious about them and every now and then examine the house through the binoculars. However, the interior of the house cannot be made out from the exterior; just as the front door remains closed, the front window curtains remain tightly drawn. Only at night can the mild light of the candle be made out through the curtains.

One Sunday morning Shanta came over and spent some time talking to me. Jocularly I asked, 'Is your husband sleeping then?'

Shyly she responded, 'Yes, he cannot sleep at night and so.....'

I remarked, 'You do not switch on the electric light at night, why is that?'

Becoming alert she answered, 'My eyes are weak, I cannot stand bright lights for a very long time. On the other hand, he cannot see in dim light. That's why, no sooner does he leave, than I switch off the electricity and light the dim lamps. You have noticed all this?'

'Yes. From morning to night, I sit by this window.'

Consolingly Shanta said, 'Truly, you can't move anywhere. Well, I will come over sometimes and also send him across.'

Things moved along in this manner. One evening, Tapan too stopped by on the way and talked with me for a while.

Then, one day deep into the night, something strange drew my attention.

Generally I go to bed at nine thirty. But, I suffer from insomnia; quite frequently I have to stay awake all night. Two weeks ago I went to bed at the usual time, but just could not get a wink of sleep. After twelve I gave up the attempt and got up; I thought that a cup of cocoa might make me sleepy.

Lighting the stove, I put the water to boil. Ramdhin sleeps in front of the door to my room, but I did not wake him.

It was a winter evening and the windows were closed. Suddenly on an impulse I threw open the windows. It was dead of night and there was not a soul about; the light in front of the twin houses was burning. Inside both the houses it was dark.

A man approached from the opposite footpath. From head to foot he was covered in a black wrapper; he stopped in front of the twin houses and craning his head looked back and all around; then, in a flash he slipped into the alley between the twin houses. I could not see him any longer. But in a little while the electric light came on in Tapan's room and was then switched off.

Having prepared the cocoa and sipping the drink, I began to think. Who was the man? There was an impression of wary alertness about his behaviour. From the alley one can also go towards the rear door of the Madrasis. But, there were a number of them and towards the evening they would lock the doors and go to sleep; undoubtedly this man had gone to Tapan's room. Tapan is not there at night, Shanta remains alone; the man had come stealthily at this time. What was the matter!

Deep into the night, husband absent, nobody at home except a young woman; a man covered in a wrapper comes at this time. That means.........? I felt depressed. Shampa had seemed a nice girl; but these days it is difficult to assess a girl's character by looking at her face. Let it go to hell, what did it matter to me! What business of mine was it what the wives of tenants were up to? As long as I got the rent on time.

I thought of standing at the window and noting when the man left, but as I was feeling sleepy after having the cocoa I went to bed. If I ignored the incipient sleep, perhaps I would have to remain awake all night.

Two weeks passed since this incident. Last Sunday Tapan came and paid the rent and nothing momentous happened. I did not mention the nocturnal visitor to Tapan. What need was there?

Then, suddenly the incident of the night of the day before yesterday.

The day before yesterday night too I was struck by insomnia. Tossing and turning till midnight I got up. Putting the water to boil for the cocoa, I opened the window and peeped out. It was almost as though he was waiting for me to peep out–the wrapper covered man. Rapidly walking along the footpath, just at the mouth of the alley, he hid himself inside. Then, from the same direction I saw another man approaching. Coming to the entrance of the alley, the man with a comforter wrapped around his neck came to an abrupt halt—uncertainly he began to look this side and that. It seemed that he had been following the wrapper covered man and now could no longer see him.

At this time the wrapper covered man removed the wrapper from his face. To my amazement I recognized—Tapan! In a moment a calamity took place. A knife flashed in Tapan's hands and with one leap, he drove the knife into the man's chest. The man fell on the footpath. Like a flash of lightening Tapan disappeared into the alley.

Dumbstruck I kept staring. The man lay motionless on the footpath and did not emit even a whisper. Must have died.

I have a telephone in my room. Getting over the shock, I called up the Police Station. Our station is very close by and the police came over in five minutes. Listening to my statement, the inspector also surrounded Tapan's house.

However, Tapan was not found at home. Shanta was sleeping and was not aware of what had happened. There was no doubt that Tapan had entered the house using the rear door. He had surreptitiously changed his clothes at home and without waking Shanta had quietly absconded.

That night the corpse was not identified; later on it was revealed that the dead man's name was Bibhutibhushan Aich, an employee of the Burdwan Police who had recently come to Kolkata on leave.

The police have posted a guard in front of Tapan's house. He has still not been apprehended by the police. The officers are continually interrogating Shanta. But, poor girl, she is innocent. I am ashamed of wrongly having suspected her. Now I have understood that it was Tapan who would return home at midnight, covered in a wrapper.

I am in a pathetic condition. I have no idea why Tapan has committed murder, every hour police officers turn up to interrogate me. I am a helpless cripple, but the police suspect that I am probably responsible for the killing. My crime is that Tapan is my client and I have witnessed the murder.

Now, my humble request to you is—please rescue me; I am being hounded at every turn. On grounds of suspicion, maybe the police will clap me into prison; then I will die. I have money; if you rescue me, I will see to it that you are not unhappy.

What else is there to say? As soon as you can, please rescue me from this harassment by the police. I will remain ever grateful to you.

Yours obediently
Sri Chintamani Kundu

TWO

Byomkesh took the letter from my hands and began reading it himself. I moved towards the kitchen in search of another cup of tea. Perhaps Satyabati was still angry–she would also have to calmed.

Returning after half an hour, I found Byomkesh with the letter on his lap, laughing to himself. I asked, 'Why the laughter?'

Byomkesh replied, 'The matter is laughable. But, Chintamani Kundu has made one mistake–he did not notice the correct time when the lights went off in Tapan's room.'

"How did you know?"

"If my assumptions are correct, then he has definitely made a mistake. He has also made another mistake, but that is absolutely natural." Byomkesh once again gave that mocking smile. Then, growing serious he said, 'Ajit, there is a telephone in Chintamani Babu's room. Find out his number and give him a call. An answer is needed to an urgent question. Ask him what sort of a voice Tapan has."

"Definitely an urgent question! Do you want to know anything more?"

"Nothing else. Tell him not to worry, I am coming immediately."

After phoning Chintamani Babu, I returned with his answer "Tapan has a rasping kind of voice."

Byomkesh responded, "Rasping! Then I am right, there is no mistake."

I said, "What you are right about only you know. But, even Chintamani Babu's voice seemed rasping to me."

Byomkesh said, "What's so surprising about that? Paralysis and on top of it being terrorised by the police—come on, let's make a move. We can have lunch after returning."

The road to Chintamani Babu's house was new and quite broad; being situated absolutely at the end, it was relatively deserted. It was easy to identify Tapan Sen's house by the police guards all around. Opposite it was Chintamani Babu's two-storied house. We went upstairs.

Before we could knock at the door, the Hindustani[6] servant Ramdhin opened the door and stood aside. We entered. Chintamani Babu was sitting beside the open window, eagerly he craned his neck forward and said, "Byomkesh Babu, I recognized you from the road itself. Come in."

Ramdhin brought forward two chairs and we took our seats. The image I had formed of Chintamani Babu's looks from the telephonic voice was in reality not so; he was a dark, plump kind of man, and while seated, did not appear to be paralysed. On a teapoy[7] beside him was a pair of expensive binoculars.

---

6 **Hindustani:** Usually referring to a non-Bengali, probably from the state of Bihar.
7 **Teapoy:** A kind of small side table.

Chintamani Babu said, "First of all tell me, what will you have–tea, cocoa, ovaltine?"

Byomkesh answered, "Nothing is needed right now. Did the police visit you today?"

Chintamani Babu said, "Didn't they just! The inspector once charges towards me and once towards Shanta in that house. What they want I just do not understand. The same questions fifty times! I am paralysed, whether I can climb down the stairs or not, why I have kept binoculars and why have I let a house to Tapan Sen? Tell me Byomkesh Babu, what answers can I possibly give to these questions? Continually answering has left me half dead. Now, please save me."

Byomkesh said, "Don't worry, everything will be fine. Now, I have to meet the police officer once. Is he........"

As he was speaking, the police officer came and stood in front of the door.

Ten years ago, when Bijoy Bhaduri had been a petty constable, we had been first introduced. Looking like a tall, thin bamboo, he was an extremely capable and suspicious man by nature. It is true that in ten years he had become a senior officer, but his appearance remained just the same. That his mind remained just as prone to suspicion as previously, could be made out from the look in his eyes.

Looking at us keenly from the doorway, he entered the room and in dry tones said, "I see it is Byomkesh Babu!"

Smiling Byomkesh said, "Then you do recognize me! So, has your criminal, meaning Tapan Sen, been apprehended?"

Casting a sharp look at Chintamani Babu, Bijoy Bhaduri said, "He has not been caught as yet, but where will he

Incomparable 55

escape? What is the purpose of your sudden visit here, Byomkesh Babu?"

Byomkesh replied, "Chintamani Babu is my client. There has been a murder in his house, his tenant has murdered; you all are bothering him. So, in order to protect his interests he has engaged me."

Frowning, Bijoy Bhaduri continued to stare at Byomkesh, probably deciding whether to have him thrown out or not. Then when he spoke, he sang a completely different tune. Leaning towards Byomkesh, in mild tones he said, "Will you step out for a moment? I have something to say."

"Come on then."

We went and stood in a corner of the long verandah outside the room. Bijoy Babu said, "Look Byomkesh Babu, you are well connected in the upper echelons, if you want to interfere in this case, I cannot do a thing. But, I am requesting you, please do not help Chintamani Kundu. I believe he and that Khotta servant of his are involved in this matter."

Byomkesh quietly listened to what Bijoy Babu had to say. Then he asked, "Do you know who has committed the murder?"

Bijoy Babu responded, "Of course it is Tapan Sen who is the murderer, but that old man is also involved."

"If that old man was involved, then, would he have brought about a murder charge against Tapan?"

"That's where the cunning lies. He wants to get Tapan involved and escape himself."

Irritated, Byomkesh answered, "Excuse me Bijoy Babu, you have not understood a thing about this case."

Frowning, Bijoy Babu asked, "Meaning?"

Byomkesh said, "The meaning I will explain later. First of all, why don't you answer some of my questions. Has the knife with which the murder was committed been found?"

"No, Tapan has absconded with it."

"Has anything been found after searching Tapan's house?"

"No, no clue which will lead to his being traced. But the safe has not yet been opened–the key is with Tapan."

"Has Shanta's investigation revealed anything?"

"Nothing worthwhile. They have been married for about four months; Shanta does not know anything about her husband's work."

"Hmn! But I know everything. I know who has committed the murder; as a matter of fact, I even know where the accused is hiding."

Bijoy Babu leaped up, "If you know, why haven't you said anything so far?"

Byomkesh smiled, "When its time, all will be revealed. Before that I want to move about and have a look at Tapan's house. Also, I want to ask Shanta a few questions. Of course, you have questioned her enough and also received satisfactory answers. I only want to ask a couple of questions."

Bijoy Babu said, "That's fine, but the criminal......."

"You will also get the criminal."

"Where? In this house? I cannot understand a word of what you are saying."

"You will. Lets go to that house first. Be prepared to nab the criminal."

"Meaning—you mean to say that Tapan Sen will return home or, is hiding in the house itself?"

"Come along, come along..." Byomkesh led the way towards the stairs. In front of Chintamani Babu's room he paused, "Chintamani Babu, don't worry. We are going to that house for a while. The murder mystery will be solved in an hour."

Then, we came down the stairs.

Tapan's house was packed with police. I have noticed a strange matter–the police become extremely alert once a thief has absconded. It is beyond my comprehension—what is the use of putting the police on strict guard when the thief has already taken to his heels. Moving down the alley towards the rear door, Byomkesh said, "Is there any other door besides the front and rear, by which one can escape? Can't one cross the boundary wall and run away?"

Daroga[8] Bijoy Babu said, "No."

One police was on guard at the rear door and in addition the door was locked. On Bijoy Babu's orders the guard unlocked the door and we entered.

Two rooms at the side of a small courtyard, adjoining was the kitchen and bathroom. Byomkesh said, "Bijoy Babu, you and Ajit go and sit with Shanta, while I have a look at the bathroom and kitchen," saying which he went off to one side.

We entered the front room. This was the sitting room. Shanta was sitting on a wicker chair, helpless and melancholic. It was an accurate description that Chintamani Kundu had given of her looks; presently her hair was unkempt; eyes were puffy. Probably she had been crying.

---

8 **Daroga:** Police officer.

She looked up as we entered the room. Not even noticing me, she gazed questioningly at Bijoy Babu. Not saying a word Bijoy Babu sat down on a chair. I too seated myself.

The three of us sat in silence. I thought to myself–the police interrogation must have tired out the girl. If she was innocent, even if she had no connection with her husband's crime, she would still have no respite. But why did Tapan murder that man? A sex crime? Did Shanta...... that man?!

Byomkesh entered from the bedroom; he was smiling. He pulled up a chair before Shanta and steadily looked at her face.

Shanta too tiredly looked at him; then, gradually, her face turned wary and worried. She sat up straight and said, "What, what?"

In cheerful tones Byomkesh said, "I saw a small iron safe in your bedroom. What does it contain?"

Shanta said, "I have already told Daroga Babu, I don't know. My husband kept the key to the safe with himself."

Bijoy Babu said, "I have made arrangements to break open the lock of the safe."

"Good, good, you will get a lot of stuff there; stolen goods, jewellery of the afternoon dacoities." Byomkesh turned towards Shanta, "Tell me, didn't your husband shave? There isn't any shaving equipment at home."

Shanta turned pale and in indistinct tones said, "He used to shave in the saloon."

Byomkesh said, "Oh, I see, your husband was an extraordinary man. He would shave in a saloon and yet not wear shoes or slippers at home. Was there any reason?"

Lowering her eyes Shanta said, "His slippers were torn and we had not got around to getting another pair. At home he would use my slippers."

Byomkesh said, "Really? Then you both have the same size?"

Shanta answered, "Yes, almost."

Byomkesh responded, "That's great. So very convenient! I see that you–husband and wife share a lot of similarities, only the hair colour is different. Chintamani Babu had informed us that Tapan's hair colour was copperish. Is that right?"

Shanta swallowed, "Yes."

Bijoy Babu had been listening to this entire conversation, with eyes popping out; suddenly standing up and in extremely agitated tones he said, "Byomkesh Babu!"

Byomkesh raised his hand and said, "Wait. Be prepared, now comes my last question. Shanta Devi[9], Chintamani Babu had noticed a reddish mole on your cheek, where has that gone?"

Shanta all of a sudden put up her hand to her left cheek and then, controlling herself said, "Mole! I don't have any mole on my cheek, Chintamani Babu must have made a mistake. Maybe there had been a red ink mark."

A hard smile lit up Byomkesh's face. He said, "I see you have prepared answers to all the questions. But, what answer do you have for this!" In a flash he tugged at Shanta's hair and the false hair-do came away revealing a copper coloured crew cut.

Shanta too responded like lightening. Bending slightly she picked up the edge of the sari from her right foot. A sleek, sharp knife was attached to her foot with a garter. Skilfully

---

9 **Devi:** This suffix is usually added to a lady's first name while addressing her.

grasping the knife in her fist, Shanta aimed it at Byomkesh's throat. Frightened and as if hypnotized, I could only stare unblinkingly. It is unimaginable how the soft and gentle face of a woman can change in an instance to such ugly hardness.

If Daroga Bijoy Babu had not been prepared, it is doubtful whether Byomkesh's life could have been saved; he leaped forward like a tiger and grasped Shanta's wrist; the knife fell to the floor.

Shanta shot a poisonous look at Byomkesh and like a venomous snake ready to strike, began to breathe deeply.

With a smiling face Byomkesh stood up, "Bijoy Babu, here is your murderous criminal and here is the murder weapon!"

Somewhat hesitantly Bijoy Babu said, "But Chintamani Babu had said, Tapan Sen........"

Byomkesh said, "Tapan Sen does not have an existence, Bijoy Babu. The only one who does is the incomparable Shanta Sen. She truly is a great soul. Do not assume that killing Bibhutibhusan Aich is the only achievement to her credit. About two months ago she had escaped from Burdwan Jail by killing a guard. I do not know her actual name; you belong to the police, you might be knowing the escaped convict's name."

Grasping Shanta with an iron hand, with eyes like gimlets Bijoy Babu stared at her face; he spat out the words, "Pramila Pal! Now I have understood everything. You had been sentenced to life imprisonment for poisoning your husband. After two years you had escaped from jail by killing the guard. After that you had hidden here, disguising yourself as both husband and wife. Then, that night Bibhutibhushan had spotted you. Having recognized you, he followed you. You murdered him here, in front of the house." Turning to Byomkesh, Bijoy Babu said, "Well, isn't all this true?"

Byomkesh said, "More or less, yes."

Bijoy Babu called out loudly, "Jamadaar[10]!"

The Jamadaar was right outside, he entered. Bijoy Babu said, "Put on the handcuffs ."

Sipping at a cup of tea in Chintamani Babu's room, Byomkesh said, "A doubt struck me on reading your letter, Chintamani Babu. You had never seen them together, in spite of using binoculars, you could not penetrate their protected boundary. Why? The man was short, the girl was tall—absolutely different. They did not use the front door, but rather the rear for their movements; the man talked in a rasping voice. Why? A suspicion arose that something was being hidden somewhere.

"But, there is no need to go into elaborate details. In broad outlines the matter stands thus—Pramila Pal needed two things after absconding from jail; she needed disguise and an income. Her hair was of a copperish hue, which easily attracted attention; so, she had to trim her hair and become a man. But to commit dacoity in the afternoon, she needed to be a woman; so she bought herself an expensive foreign wig. Where she had her hair cut and where she organized the wig from I do not know; but, then began her dual life. Now its winter and very easy for a woman to disguise herself as a man. She fixed a small butterfly moustache below her nose, put on an overcoat over her coat and pants and then came to rent the house from you. Just in case feminine tones

---

10 **Jamadaar:** Here referring to a police guard.

surfaced she talked to you in a rasping voice. Its very easy to remain disguised in Kolkata, nobody in the locality bothers to keep track of anyone. But she observed that you were always by your window and you had binoculars. She would have to be very careful.

"That night, after you retired, she came with all her luggage to occupy the room. Nobody was any wiser that only one person had shifted in instead of two. She had a small iron safe with her, which she placed in the bedroom.

"Then began her daily routine. In the morning she would leave on the pretext of going to school; in the afternoon she would move about trying to organize the 'afternoon dacoities' and then return in the evening. Again in the evening she would leave, dressed as a man, to deceive you. Switching off the electricity, she would light a lamp and go out; when the oil finished, the lamp went out and you thought that Shanta had put the lights and gone to sleep. You had made only one mistake; you did not notice that the electric lights were switched off before Tapan left the house. Since you did not suspect, you did not notice.

"Anyway, after you went to bed, she would return and go to sleep. She probably tied some warm clothing around her waist—while returning, she would cover herself with that. So, the first night you spotted her while opening the window, you assumed she was Shanta's secret lover.

"Matters continued in this manner, Then, suddenly great danger befell Shanta. Bibhutibhushan was a police employee. He had seen Pramila before, coming to Kolkata for his holiday, he ran into Pramila and recognized her. He began to follow

Pramila. Maybe they had both met at some hotel. Pramila must have tried to shake him off, but when she couldn't..."

Leaving the sentence incomplete, Byomkesh stopped; taking out a cigarette he lit it.

I said, "One point, why did Pramila not run away after killing Bibhutibhishan?"

Byomkesh replied, "She did not get the time to escape. She did not know that Chintamani Babu had witnessed the murder through the window. So, she was not in any great hurry; she had thought that she would put together all the expensive jewellery and escape at leisure. It was no longer safe for her to remain in that house; the corpse was in front of her house, the police would definitely interrogate her. Pramila Pal was a convict who had broken free from gaol, what if someone from the police recognized her? She definitely would have run. But, suddenly within five minutes, the police surrounded the house. Then there was no opportunity to escape, Pramila quickly put on her wig, turning into a girl. But in her hurry, she forgot to sketch on the mole."

"Why did she sketch a mole on her cheek?"

"To highlight the difference in the two appearances. As a man she sported a butterfly moustache beneath her nose and as a woman, besides her wig, she sketched a mole. Understood? Now please allow us to take our leave, Chintamani Babu."

Along with gushing thanks, Chintamani Babu wrote out a cheque for two hundred rupees.

It was getting on to be two 'o'clock. The police had disappeared with the convict. Srijukta[11] Bijoy Bhaduri must

---

11 **Srijukta:** A polite form of 'Mister.'

have won wide acclaim and praise for arresting the murderous criminal.

Reaching home, we found Satyabati waiting anxiously by the door; seeing us she raised her eyebrows questioningly, as if to say 'Why so late?"

Byomkesh suddenly laughed out aloud. Then, reaching out and chucking Satyabati gently under the chin, he said, "You all too are no less, my dear!"

Why?

I had lived for a while in a city of Uttaranchal[1]. Situated on the banks of the Ganges, there were a few Bengali families. But for me, I had come close to only one Bengali, Nrisingha Pal. He used to live right next door to me, in a small house.

There could be few with as repulsive an appearance as Nrisingha Babu. A bestial gorilla–like face, small cunning eyes; all the hair on his head had turned white, yet stood upright like the needles of a porcupine. He was probably near about sixty, yet physically as strong as a demon. The first day I had seen him, my heart had leapt up in fright!

Perhaps due to his physical appearance or whatever reason, he did not have too much interaction with others. Twice a day, in the morning and evening, he would go to bathe in the Ganges; but besides that did not emerge from the house. I did not observe anyone go to his house either other than a character by the name of 'Lame Manik', under the cover of the darkness of the night.

---

11 **Uttaranchal:** The northern section of the country is referred to here.

I remained busy with my studies and did not try to further an acquaintance with Nrisingha Babu. If his physical appearance mirrored his character, it was better not to get too close. But one day he himself came forward to make friends. My servant had run away; rather helplessly I was reflecting that if this was my plight when a servant absconded, what was the sense in being independent, when Nrisingha Babu turned up and said, "The menial has run away! Don't worry, I'll arrange for a new one tomorrow. Today my servant will come and do all your work."

Nrisingha Babu had a full-throated and sweet voice; rather like the piping of the shehnai[2]. It did not seem to be in accordance with the physique.

Thereafter, an intimacy grew with him. He bathed in the Ganges twice a day–yet, partook of no religious ceremonies; broached no devotional topics–all in all it seemed rather amazing. His physical appearance I had gradually got used to; but whether his character was good or not still remained undecided. Maybe he was a secret drinker, perhaps there were other faults too; but, one thing I had noticed–he never wanted to hurt anybody and seeing anyone in distress he would try his utmost to help out. He had no wife, child or relative and lived all alone.

One evening, in the course of taking a stroll, I found that I had strayed far from home. It was a winter evening, with not too many people on the roads; I had reached a point where three or four roads merged–and was undecided as to

---

2 **Shehna:** A piped musical instrument with sonorous and hauntingly melodious notes.

which one would lead me home when I saw Nrisingha Babu returning home after bathing in the Ganges. He was barefooted, a light covering on his body and in his hands was some wet clothing wrapped in a towel. Both of us walked back side by side. I had not been in this part before and asked, "How far are the banks of the Ganges from here?"

"About a mile."

"You come here twice a day?"

"Yes."

A bit surprised I asked, "There are other banks close by, why don't you go there?"

He said, "This is attached to the cemetery and I come here."

Suddenly it occurred to me—was he then a Kapalik[3]? But, where were the Rudraksha[4] beads, where was the vermilion[5] marking his forehead? There was nothing of that sort.

We walked in silence for a while. It had turned quite dark, besides which there were tall trees by the roadside. A sliver of a moon could be seen in the sky, but it did not suffice in penetrating the darkness of the night.

My attention was drawn to the fact that while walking Nrisingha Babu would sometimes turn around and look back. I asked, "What are you looking at?"

---

3 **Kapalik:** An ascetic practicing religion through certain occult rites and generally regarded somewhat warily.
4 **Rudraksha:** Seeds of a particular tree, used as prayer beads.
5 **Vermilion:** Red powder-like substance generally worn by married women in the parting of the hair and also used in some religious ceremonies.

"Just take a look and see if someone is following us!"

Suddenly a chill ran down my spine. I glanced back keenly and replied, "Why, no!"

"Can you hear any sound?"

"No, what is the matter?"

"Nothing. A couple of months ago two dogs from the cemetery had killed a Muslim thug by tearing open his throat at this very spot."

Ten minutes later we reached the locality and a further five minutes after that, our neighbourhood. Nrisingha Babu's house was before mine; he said, "Come in and have some tea."

In his living room a carpet was spread out over the couch. We sat facing each other and sipping hot tea. A lot of questions about Nrisingha Babu surfaced once more. What sort of a person was he? How much parity was there between his exterior and interior? Why was I unable to gauge the man even after such a long association?

Nrisingha Babu suddenly laughed aloud. Just like his voice, his laughter sounded like the lilting notes of a flute; when he smiled, all his teeth were fully visible.

Curbing his laughter he said, "You have made out what a wicked person I am!"

Embarrassed I responded, "No, no what are you saying...............!"

Very simply he said, "You are right! Truly, I am extremely wicked, at least I was, about three ago. Perhaps there is now a change in my mentality; but my appearance has not changed—it remains the same."

Nrisingha Babu said all this quite impassively, but I was extremely disconcerted; bringing the cup of tea to my lips,

I tried to cover up my awkwardness. He continued saying, "Mighty Nature set me forth after putting on me the hallmark of my true temperament, and I did not let her down either. There is nothing so vile that I have not done, Jagai-Madhai[6] were babes in arms compared to me. Life was continuing in this manner, then one day, thanks to a very minor incident everything turned topsy-turvy. Do not assume my mentality changed or I became saintly overnight. My point of view has not changed all that much, in truth it is this living world that has been transformed. You will be astounded to hear this—that is what I will tell you today."

"Carry on."

There was a slight interruption at this point. The outer door was closed, someone's light touch pushed it open and a man peeped inside. The skeletal visage covered with a fur cap was weasel-shaped; the timid eyes were full of cunning. Immediately on seeing me, the face disappeared in the darkness. It was like a strange mongrel peeping into the kitchen in the hope of food and making an escape on seeing people inside.

Startled I asked, "Who was that?"

Nrisingha Babu laughed, "No ghost or spirit—a human. He is known as 'Lame Manik', a creature of the night. Sometimes he comes to call on me."

"But why did he run away?"

---

6 **Jagai-Madhai:** These two were known for their extremely villainous nature, but after coming into contact with the great religious leader Sri Chaitanya, they reformed.

"Seeing you he took to his heels. He visits me in stealth. There is an extremely wealthy person in this city by the name of Ramnehal Singh; Lame Manik is his stooge. If Ramnehal comes to know that Lame Manik visits me, he will have him chopped into little bits. Let that be—let me get on with the story."

Nrisingha Babu locked the front door and came and sat down.

"I was a daroga[7] with the police. Joining as a Writer Constable I rose to the post of Senior Constable. Could have gone even higher, but deliberately did not do so. There is no fun in the upper echelons.

"In the police force, there was no officer more fiery than I—even now probably there isn't. I had a scheming intelligence and was extremely adept at working within the loopholes of the law. Anyone in my clutches would be turned inside out before being set free. Thieves, unruly characters, the wicked and the depraved feared me, gentlemen were more scared. People in whatever district I was transferred to, would become positively distraught. The wealthy would on their own initiative come and shower me with money so that my attention was not focused on them.

"In this manner, I was in my element. I had not married; with a mentality like mine it would be stupid to do so. The salary was measly, but the extras overflowed. I am living off that income now—even if I am to live for another twenty years, the money will not come to an end.

---

7 **Daroga:** Police officer.

"Externally feared like a wild beast, internally living in a surfeit of liquor and good food. I got whatever I wanted and lived in the highest of spirits.

"About eight years ago, the Officer-in-Charge of an important police station was transferred here. It is a rich city, abounding in the wealthy. People sat up and gifts began to be stealthily sent across. The greater the filth, the greater the richness of the gift. Only one person did not send a thing-it was that Ramnehal Singh. He had his own estates and also ran a business of money lending and was fabulously well-off. He remained stubbornly adamant and gave nothing.

"About a month later, on the pretext of a minor errand I turned up at his house. By indication I gave him to understand that I wanted money. He told me to my face, 'I have seen innumerable policemen like you—do whatever you can, the S.P. is in my hands.'

"I returned fuming and ready to burst. Just you wait and see–is the S.P. more effective or is Narsingh Daroga!"

"I began weaving a web. It is not particularly difficult to entangle these landowners in one or the other legal imbroglio, some small case or the other is always at hand. But I had decided that Ramnehal Singh would be dealt such a blow that he would never again be able to raise his head. I would snap his backbone.

"Lame Manik, whom you have just seen was even then Ramnehal's stoodge. He was the one who would execute all the dirty tasks of Ramnehal. One day I got hold of him. Did not haul him to the police station, I took him home and gave him to understand that for all that he had done, I could have him sentenced for ten years on five counts. Lame Manik fell at my feet.

"Since that time Lame Manik has been my private eye. At night, stealthily, he would keep me intimated of Ramnehal's secrets. I had put the fear of God into him to such an extent that he is still scared. I no longer have a job and have no power either; but he believes that should I so desire, I can have him thrown into jail whenever I want. So he drops in once in a while and keeps me posted with the news.

"Let that be. For one and a half year, steadily I built up a case. Not a case, it was a work of art. Ramnehlal's son was then about nineteen or twenty. He had killed a common prostitute. Witnesses papers-everything was so watertight that there was no loophole to escape.

"Ramnehal's son was sentenced for fourteen years–the S.P. could not save him. Only his youth saved him from being hanged. That boy is still rotting in jail.

"From this one example you can gauge what sort of a person I am. A few years went by and it was time for me to retire. I had made a lot of money, there was no need for me to work. I could have applied for an extension, but did not.

"I had bought this small home. Wrapping up all work, I came and settled down here. My heart filled with conceit–whatever I had wanted I had got, had been defeated by none. What else was there to desire!

"That day, I sat down in this very room with a bottle of liquor; the whole night I would celebrate all by myself. A pistol full of bullets was at my side. I had a lot of enemies. Whoever came to settle scores because I had retired, would be dealt with.

"Engrossed, I continued to drink. There was no keeping track of time. Suddenly looking up, I found a frightful apparition before me–an emaciated sanyasi[8]; coiled locks atop the head, a vermilion mark on his forehead and the entire body covered with ash.

"Through force of habit I grabbed the pistol but the sadhu harshly chided me, 'Put down the gun!'

"What an impact, it sounded like staccato gunfire. It is unbelievable but the pistol dropped down from my hands and I looked on like a sheep.

"The sanyasi then said, 'Your time has come. You will bathe in the Ganges twice everyday. Think of the Divine Mother. No more drinking and you will not shave on Wednesdays.'

"I burst into raucous laughter. As it is I was drunk and on top of that, not shave on Wednesdays! All that continual laughter for such a long while left me breathless. All of a sudden it occurred to me–the front door was locked, then how did the sanyasi enter? I stopped laughing and looking around, found that the sanyasi had left. But the door remained bolted as before.

"That is why I had said it is not my perspective that has changed but the world. Everything impossible and absurd began to take place, what cannot happen, should not happen began to happen.

"That night I had fallen asleep here itself. Towards dawn, hearing a knocking on the front door, I woke up. I thought that someone was playing the fool with me. My hangover had not cleared then, and I did not even remember the sanyasi. Picking up the pistol and tiptoeing to the front door, I suddenly

---

8 **Sanyasi:** Holy man.

flung it open. I found nobody there but a man walking rapidly away along the road.

"The stubborn streak in me surfaced–and I set out in hot pursuit. Bare feet, clutching a pistol, I followed the man. In the light of the dawn, the surroundings were not clearly visible; however fast I walked he walked faster; I began running, so did he.

"After running for quite a distance, I could no longer see him. So far I had not been aware of where I was going. Now, waking up from the stupor with a jerk I found I was on the banks of the Ganges. Near the cemetery.

"The banks near the cemetery were empty. Standing there, all alone, the words of the sanyasi came back to me. He had said–Bathe in the Ganges twice a day. It was summer and running all that way, I was sweating profusely. I thought to myself–"What's the harm? Might as well bathe and go back." I returned after bathing in the Ganges.

"That day was Wednesday, but I did not remember. At eight 'o' clock I went to shave. I shave myself, not trusting a barber. But I managed to cut myself and began bleeding copiously. Then I remembered it was Wednesday and the sanyasi had instructed me not to shave on Wednesday.

"Damm! What did it matter if I didn't shave for a day. My body burned in anger. A beggar had come and hypnotized me! No, never! I was Narsingh Daroga–criminals and the law-abiding alike were subdued in sheer terror of me, and a sanyasi would lead me by a ring through my nose! One would have to check the strength of his power.

"But I could do nothing. After evening, I was about to sit with a entire bottle of brandy when it slipped from my hands and shattered into bits. There was no more alcohol in the house, but I wouldn't acknowledge defeat. I hired a coach and set out for the liquor shop.

"The liquor shop was closed. Went to another one, that too was shut. The liquor vendors had apparently gone on strike.

"On returning to the coach the driver asked, 'Sir, where to now?' I answered, "To hell."

"The coach left and I continued to simmer with anger. When the coach stopped, I found I was on the banks of the river beside the cemetery. I returned after a bath.

"This continued for a few days. I no longer seemed to have any will of my own; I had to bathe twice daily in the Ganges and could not partake of liquor; could not shave on Wednesday. I was not a free man, but a bought slave. My unknown master taking me by the scruff of the neck rubbed my nose in the dust.

"One day, losing all my patience I said to myself, Ma,[9] I don't believe in you, don't accept wily tricks. But if falling in with Sanyasi's orders averts any problems, so be it. I won't drink anymore, will bathe twice a day in the Ganges and not shave on Wednesday. If someone stands to gain by that–well and good.

"Gradually I became used to bathing twice a day in the Ganges, gave up shaving on Wednesdays. But giving up drinking was not that easy. I was forced to my knees a couple of times more. Each time I attempted to drink, some danger or the other befell me. Once, I had poured out liquor in a glass when

---

9   **Ma:** Mother Goddess.

a lizard plunged into it, dropping down from the ceiling. Ultimately I gave up trying. For a few days the whole world turned drab and colourless.

"Oh well, the days continued to pass in this trouble-free manner. I remember the Divine Mother[10] that is, whenever I remembered I cursed Her profusely. Who she was I didn't know, and neither did I have any idea why She was chasing after me, but I abused Her in abundance. Probably she liked it, because no matter what I said, I came to no harm.

"One evening, Lame Manik turned up. He said, "Narsingh Babu, leave this town and go away. Ramnehal Singh has engaged hired killers to finish you off. If you remain here, you will lose your life."

"Ramnehal had engaged killers? That was not surprising. I had tarred his face and sent his son to jail–naturally he sought vengeance. But, I am Narsingh Paul–would I run away in fright of Ramnehal? I have always wrecked havoc amongst criminals, trying to use them to scare me! No matter, let the killers come. I will deal with them.

"Even then I took precautions. Whenever I went out, I carried a pistol; it remained beside my pillow while sleeping at night. At odd hours of the night, I would peep from the window to see if anyone was lurking in any odd corner. But, I could never spot a soul-it was probably all a hoax. They were misguided attempts to scare me.

"Manik turned up again after about eight days or so. Giving me a beaming smile he said, "You are truly to be congratulated,

---

10 **Mother:** Here usually addressed thus, reference once again to 'Ma'.

Why? 77

keeping your wits about you in this manner! Ramnehal has totally wilted." Astounded I exclaimed, "What's that!"

"Lame Manik said, "You have kept as pets two fierce tiger-like mastiffs, they remain guarding this house all night. The thugs turned up thrice but they were scared away. With my own ears I have heard them tell Ramnehal, "They are not dogs Sir, they are veritable messengers of death."

"I did not say a word to Lame Manik, but there was an uneasy kind of discomfort in my mind. Where did the mastiffs come from? Then I sat up on guard all night, but could not see even a stray dog.

"This was amazing! Villains could see the dogs, then why couldn't I? I thought to myself–the thugs know me and are scared to enter my house, they have spun a story to Nehal.

"The next couple of days passed without any problems. Thanks to the protective invisible guards I remained safe. The fright gradually ebbed away. Even while going to bathe in the Ganges, I did not carry my pistol. There were no more glimpses of the Sanyasi and neither did I turn pious. But within myself I sought to know the Divine Mother. I asked, "Who are You? Explain to me. My entire world has turned upside down; nothing is apparent to me. You clarify."

"But, She did not explain. The Almighty continued to enjoy herself at my expense.

"I am talking of an incident that took place six months ago. Lame Manik appeared looking wan and washed out. He asked, "Do you go to bathe near the cemetery every morning and evening?"

I replied, "Yes."

Lame Manik said, "They have come to know. The Hindu thugs have refused to kill you, claiming that you are a sorcerer, practising your craft seated on corpses in the cemetery. So, Ramnehal has engaged Muslim hoodlums. You are probably familiar with the names–Rahim and Karim, two brothers. They will knife you on the road, on the way to the cemetery."

After Lame Manik left, I sat down to reflect on what could be done. It was impossible to stop bathing in the Ganges, because I knew that if I did not go willingly, I would be dragged there by the scruff of my neck. Yes, one way out would be to carry a pistol. But, God knows why I did not any longer feel like carrying a pistol while going for a dip in the Ganges. Oh, what did it matter, whatever was to happen. Nothing was taking place the way I wanted—then, why bother worrying?

Nothing happened for a couple of days. I would go for a bath and return. I almost forgot that hoodlums had been set on me! Then one day—

You have noticed how dark it turns towards the cemetery side in the evenings. There are no houses that side and people virtually stop walking about there. I was returning after a bath, it would be about 8p.m. It had turned quite dark. All of a sudden, hearing a horrific scream at the rear, I turned around. Agonised shrieks in a human voice accompanied the deep throated growls of mastiffs. It sounded as if a hound had grasped a man by the throat and was throttling his screams.

I did not wait any longer and took to my heels.

"The next morning we got the news that the hoodlum Rahim's corpse had been found on the road to the cemetery. The cemetery dogs had apparently slaughtered him by tearing his throat to shreds. Rahim had had a spear in his hands, but even then had not been able to protect himself.

"Lame Manik turned up at night. I heard what Rahim's brother Karim had told Ramnehal. For a number of days both the brothers had lain in wait for me, every single day they had observed a pair of black dogs following me. Yesterday, both Rahim and Karim had perched on a tree by the road, their intention being to kill me with a spear as soon as I passed beneath the tree; the mastiffs would not be able to do a thing. But, as Rahim fell down while aiming the spear, a mastiff had come and caught him by the throat.

Nrisingha Babu became silent. Then, drawing a deep breath he said, "That is my story. After that Ramnehal did not interfere with me any longer. I remain relaxed and tension free since then.

"Now, you tell me—What is this all about? Just saying "Supernatural" will not do, you will have to explain the reason why. The sanyasi had said, "Your time has come." But, how is that possible? I have heard that God is merciful to those saintly people, those who meditate, and protects them from all danger. But, what is this! I have never done a jot of good in life, have been wicked in countless instances; then, what is the sense of showering me with mercy? Forcibly freeing me from a drinking habit, seeing to it that I bathe regularly in the Ganges, protecting me from enemy attacks— why all this? You are an erudite man, answer me. WHY? WHY? WHY?"

Nrisingha Babu turned a cadaverous face full of intense quest towards me. I could not answer him. Perhaps this intense heartfelt query itself was the answer to his question.

The Contrast

After having dinner together, the three friends were lounging on the carpet in the living room. In a large incense burner-like hookah bowl, fragrant tobacco perfumed the surroundings. Of the three friends, although two were Kayasthas[1] and one a Brahmin[2], yet all three shared the same hookah.

All of them were about forty years old and residents of Kolkata. Binod was a well-established doctor, in the past ten years he had built up quite a good practice. Atul and Sharat were lawyers; Atul practiced in Alipore and Sharat in the High Court. They too had made quite a name for themselves in their respective professions. All kept busy with their own work and could not meet very often though they lived close by. That day Sharat had invited his two friends over to celebrate the end of some religious fast his wife had undertaken. During the day it had not been possible and so both had turned up in the evening, when they were free.

---

1 **Kayastha:** Part of Hindu caste system—one of the higher orders, a little below that of a Brahmin.
2 **Brahmin:** The highest in the caste system.

In the course of the conversation, unknowingly the talk came to centre around the experiences of each in their respective professions. Carefully resting his elbow on the pillow and taking a deep pull on the pipe of the hookah, Atul with closed eyes said, "The deeper I delve into this profession, the more it seems that kindness, pity and religion—all of these have been eradicated from the world. Only grabbing and tearing asunder. Staying too long in this profession probably obliterates from the mind distinction between what is right and wrong. The only priority becomes—how to win the case."

Reflectively Sharat responded, "That's true. In a court, the baser side of mans' nature comes to the fore. The belief that goodness can exist becomes feeble with the non-appearance of this characteristic. In separating wheat from chaff, almost nothing appears to be left."

Atul said, "Not just appears, it truly is that way. I do not know what you all think of the matter, but it is my belief that the positive quality of 'gratitude' one only reads about in books and poetry, it has completely vanished from the face of the earth."

Laughing, Vinod remarked, "You all have become hardened cynics. That's not true. It is not good to stop believing in man, the loss is greater to one's own self."

Atul said, "Loss and gain I do not understand, I am talking of what I have observed. These days I do not even feel angry at ingratitude. Just as it is senseless mourning the loss of the Mammoth Elephant, so too this. When the truth is simply acknowledged........"

Sarat suddenly said, "I remember an incident. It has happened so many times that someone for whom we have done a favour has made only barbed remarks in return. But, God knows why, this incident has left an indelible impression on my mind."

After a moment's silence he said, "Some time back you had perhaps heard that I was leading an immoral life?"

Atul answered, "Yes, I had heard something to the effect. Someone said, 'Sarat Babu seems to have developed a pretty pair of wings these days, he is flying high!' I said—it is normal to soar these days, how is it his fault? If you have the money, you soar."

Binod smiled and said, "Such rumours had also come to my ears. I will not name any names, but such precise descriptions were given that it was difficult not to believe. Only because it is I.........."

Sarat said, "Except for the two of you and my wife, probably nobody else believed this to be anything but the absolute truth. As a matter of fact, some fair-weather friends even wanted to team up with me in the hope of good times. They thought that they had got a plump goose for the kill."

Atul asked, "What had happened?"

Sarat smiled a bit and said, "I had helped someone. The matter was so trifling that perhaps you will laugh.

"Atul, you know Netai. He practices in the Alipore bar, a junior lawyer. One cannot exactly call him a junior either—he has been practising law for ten-twelve years. Netai is distantly related to me.

"Previously they were quite well off. Netai's father earned a fat salary. But ever since his death, they had begun to hover on the edges of poverty. The only earning member of the family was Netai—and he had just started practising. So, even if I do not elaborate on the economic status, you can well imagine what it stood to be.

"Though we were related, there was no great intimacy with them, on occasions like marriages or the sacred thread ceremony, we would meet; that was the extent. About three years ago, for my sister Shanta's son annaprasan ceremony[3]. I had gone to Salkia, there I had met Netai. Not having seen him for a number of days, I was startled. The stamp of poverty seemed to be etched on his face. The boy was quite handsome and fair, but monetary problems appeared to have put a black mark on him. There always seemed to be an air of tense embarrassment about him—as though he continually wanted to hide some shameful secret.

"He came and touched my feet. I asked, 'How are you?' He replied, 'I am fine.'

"I asked, 'How is the practice coming along?' He remained silent.

"A feeling of regret overcame me. Though distantly, after all, Netai was related. If I had wanted to, couldn't I have helped him? Like Abhimanyu[4], the boy was waging a lone war to make both ends meet and was getting battered and scarred, but I remained so engrossed in my own work that I did not even have the time to look back at him!

"Mentally I resolved to do something for him. But, before that it was necessary to know what was hurting him the most.

---

3 **Annaprasan:** The ceremony in which an infant eats rice for the first time.
4 **Abhimanyu:** One of the characters of the Indian epic The Mahabharata.

The Contrast 85

Just to shower largesse on an impulse would not do. Keeping in mind that his honour and pride must also be safeguarded, and concrete help rendered–that is what had to be done.

"There was nobody else there; subtly I began to question Netai. No sooner had I asked a couple of questions in a roundabout fashion, than Netai revealed everything about his poverty. Probably because he wanted to keep everything bottled up, it all burst open.

"In the end he said, 'Its nothing else Sarat Da[5], clients do turn up every now and then and its not even that I do poor work. But, lack of one thing spoils the entire show. There are no books. You tell me, if one does not possess one's own books, would not it throw a spanner in the works? The client who turns up once, seeing my plight does not return the second time. What more can I tell you? It is impossible for me even to buy a good copy of the Civil Procedure—how will I spend thirty/thirty-five rupees at one go? After all, one will also have to eat!'

"I said, 'Will you be able to manage just by getting hold of books?"

"Restively he said, 'I think so, but as I am so unlucky...'"

"I said, 'O.K, send me a list of the books you require and I will have them sent over.'

"His eyes filled with tears and in tearful tones he said, 'Sarat Da, if you extend this help to me I will never forget it.'

"That was all that happened that day.

"The next day a lengthy list from Netai reached me. I sent it across to the Eastern Law House shop with instructions that

---

5 Da: Short form of 'Dada', meaning elder brother.

the books be sent over to Netai and I be billed. The bill came to almost eight hundred rupees.

"Then, with the pressure of work Netai completely slipped out of my mind. Suddenly about fifteen days later it occurred to me that I had got no acknowledgement of the books from Netai. I called up the Eastern Law House.

"They responded by informing me that the books had been sent across quite a while back and Netai Babu had even sent a receipt. Within half an hour a messenger came and showed me Netai's receipt.

"I thought, what has happened! Netai must have written, then has the letter been misplaced in the post? Anyway, since Netai had received the books I did not bother about it all that much.

"About a month or two after this, a whole lot of rumours and barbed jibes began reaching my ears. At first I did not pay any attention, but then the agitation grew to such an extent that one day my wife smilingly told me, "Tell me, what is all this I am hearing? You have started visiting houses of ill repute at this age!

"Where did you hear about this?"

"Hiralal Babu's wife had come over in the evening. She offered profuse sympathies!"

"I decided that enough was enough and matters could not be disregarded any longer–would have to find out where these rumours were circulating from. A great distaste began to grow in my mind. I did not meddle in anybody's affairs, consciously I had harmed none–rather to the contrary. Then, what was the profit in maligning me thus?

"It so happened that the very next evening I ran into Netai. I had not seen him since that time at Shanta's house.

He was walking along the footpath, when suddenly seeing me in front, he started as though seeing an apparition. Then, before I could say a word he retreated and seemed to take to his heels, just to get away from me.

"Matters were absolutely clear. My heart filled with bitterness and I returned home.

"Look at the fun! So long as I had done nothing for Netai, he had not spoken either good or bad of me; he was absolutely uninvolved and indifferent. But, no sooner did I extend him some help, than he began spreading rumours about me.

"Let that be. There was no longer any doubt that Netai was responsible for this; but even then, without proof and only on the basis of his demeanour he could not be pinpointed as guilty. Quite literally I began investigating.

"I came to know that a young lawyer by the name of Keshav Mitra was the most enthusiastic about these rumours. One day I cornered him in the Bar Library. A number of people were present; I asked, 'What is the matter, is this any way to behave? You have come to practice as a lawyer, haven't you taken a look at the last few pages of the penal Code?'

"With a pale face Keshav said, 'What.......what are you saying?'

"I said, 'The rumours that you are spreading about me, do you have any idea what the result can be?'

"Keshav was frightened and said, 'What can I do? If your own relative says so, is it my fault? I have not witnessed anything personally.'

"I took him aside and asked, 'Netai has said all this?'

"He said, 'Yes.'

".........Did he just say so.....Or, was there some occastion?'

"Keshav said, 'Netai is my friend. The other day I had

gone to his house and saw that you had presented him with some books. The books were delivered from the shop in front of me. Netai smiled and said, 'The books are a bribe.' Apparently he had seen you somewhere shady and this was to shut him—"

"This is what happened! I could not say anything more to Keshav and returned home only thinking about Netai."

For a long time the three were silent.

Finally Binod heaved a sigh and said, "Hmn! The world is truly filled with so many strange beings. Let me tell you of this incident. It took place many years ago, when I had just begun practicing.

"At the intersection of Mechobazaar and Badurbagan Crossing, I had opened a small dispensary. On the ground floor was the dispensary and I lived in the two rooms above. Had not married at the time and the whole world lay at my feet. I was the prince of some fairy tale; who could say what somnolent palace I would storm into and clasp which princess to my breast? A very appealing mystery lay shrouded in the mists of an unknown future, as if just refusing to give herself up. Like a playful sweetheart it smiled and vanished no sooner did I attempt to grasp it. Those were the days, what do you say, Atul?

"Oh well...the days passed quite well. The dispensary was also quite successful. All of a sudden riots broke out between the Marwaris[6] and the Muslims. Nothing momentous, one morning Hindus and Muslims woke up and started slitting each others throats.

---

6 **Marwari**: The community belonging originally to Rajasthan.

The Contrast 89

"I see no necessity of describing those atrocities, you all were also in Kolkata at the time and have had some little experience. About three murders took place in front of my dispensary, but I could not do a thing. It was a Muslim area and I was a Hindu; in such circumstances it was safest to underplay the fact of belonging to the Hindu religion as far as possible. However, I evinced some courage by keeping the dispensary open and distributing medicines to Hindus and Muslims alike. Otherwise I would not have been able to face myself.

"That locality had a hoodlum by the name of Noor Miyan[7]. Beginning from the police to the local dogs, everybody knew him. There was probably not a second man more ruthless than him in the city of Kolkata. He had about three wives—all forcibly wrested from middle-class families. Openly he carried on a trade in cocaine, but none dared accost him.

"At the time of the riots, Noor Miyan would hide in an alley close to my dispensary. If the road happened to be isolated and a Hindu was passing by, he would silently come up and with a knife about one and a half feet in length, stab him in the back and push it through the stomach. No sooner was the knifing complete than Noor Miyan would disappear. This would be followed by screams and shouts, police whistles and the sound of the ambulance. Once the wounded man was shifted, the place was silent once again.

"After a few such unexplained murders had taken place, people virtually stopped walking about in that area. Noor

---

7 **Miyan:** A term of address used by the Muslim community, equivalent to Mister.

Miyan waited in the alley, but no prey turned up. When they did come, it was armed with sticks and swords and in groups—like hunters. So, Noor Miyan and his compatriots went underground. When the latter departed, the former again emerged.

"Two days passed in this manner. The riots carried on in much the same manner. From a distance we could hear the turbulent shouts, but our locality remained quiet. Noor Miyan did not have any work at all in hand. That evening I too was sitting quietly by the window, when, hearing the sound of heavy footsteps, I peeped out and saw a *Khotta*[8] from the west, sporting a pair of heavy decorative shoes, walking rapidly forward. He was well wrapped in a shawl and from his tonsured head hung a long tuft of hair—as though a flag fluttering in the breeze. This sight made me shrink in fright. Oh no! Noor Miyan was sure to appear with his one and a half feet knife.

"That is exactly what happened. No sooner had he reached my house, when appearing from behind, Noor Miyan pounced on him like a wolf. But in seconds something momentous happened. The tuft sporting Khotta suddenly whipped around and pulled out both hands from beneath the shawl—and in both were two knives. Noor Miyan's knife remained in the hand; like lightening the Khotta had driven a knife into his chest and the other in his stomach. Then, just like he had come, well wrapped, he disappeared.

---

8 **Khotta:** A non-Bengali, usually referring to a person belonging to Bihar.

The Contrast 91

"Groaning, Noor Miyan fell to the footpath. Then, crawling he somehow dragged himself and collapsed in front of my door. The doorpost became a mess of slush and blood.

"My compounder and I somehow carried him inside. I felt–let the scoundrel die there; it was the richly deserved result of his past actions. Let me choke in the mud and atone for his sins! But, being a doctor, I just could not do that.

"Examining the wounds I found that the one on the chest was not that serious, but the stomach wound was grievous. Anyway, after giving first-aid for the time being, I was about to phone for the ambulance, when Noor Miyan opened his eyes and said, 'Doctor Sahib!'

"No sooner had I come close when he said, 'Save my life, I will give you a lakh of rupees'

"Irritated I answered, 'That is exactly what I am trying to do! Go to the Medical College and see if they can save you.'

"Pleadingly Noor Miyan said, 'Don't send me to the Mitia College[9] Babu, those Hindu doctors will poison me, they will kill me.'

"I mocked him, 'Most definitely. All the doctors of the Mitia College are like you, that's why. But, can't I also poison you and kill you? I too am a Hindu!'

"—'You will never do something like that,' saying which Noor Miyan became senseless. There had been such a lot of bloodshed that he did not have the strength to talk anymore."

"On thinking over, I also felt that with too much movement, he would die on the road itself. Helplessly I informed the hospital and took him to my house.

---

9 **Mitia College:** The Medical College colloquially referred to.

"There is perhaps nothing more astounding than man's mind. The man for whom I felt an endless disgust, a man whom I had seen committing three or four murders with my own eyes—why I kept him with me, and nursing him night and day brought him back to health, I do not know even now. While my mind wanted to poison him, I fed him pomegranate juice. In the throes of a delirium, when he had shouted out 'Kill! Kill those Hindus,' I had applied an ice bag to his forehead. You all delve into human psychology—perhaps you will be able to find a proper answer to this. Man's corporeal body is my line of work—so these subtleties have remained a mysterious puzzle to me.

"The day his fever left him, he sat up in bed and the first words he uttered were, 'Give me some cocaine.'

"From then on every day he began begging and pleading for cocaine—I would refuse and he too remained adamant.

"One day he said, 'Doctor Sahib, I will give you ten thousand rupees, give me one marking of cocaine.'

"I said, 'That I will, but let me see your money first!'

"He said, 'On my honour, I will send it over.'

"I said, 'That's enough of jokes. Know this much, not even an iota of cocaine will I give you, even for a lakh of rupees.'

"Another day when he was desperate for some cocaine, I told him, 'Noor Miyan, with my own eyes I have seen you commit two-three murders. What if I inform the police now?'

"Disdainfully he wrinkled up his nose and said, 'Nothing will happen. I have an alibi and only you will get caught up in all this.'

"I asked, 'How?'

"He said, 'During the riots I was in jail. If you do not believe me, go and check in the police station, you will even find my thumb print there.'

"The man's cunning stunned me anew. Building up an unbreakable alibi—making all preparations, he had ventured on his exploits.

"Then one day, when he had not yet recovered his strength and looked like a ghost, I told him, 'Your wounds have healed, if you want, you can leave now.'

Without another word he got up from the bed and stumbling and swaying, left. Before leaving, he bent low and saluted me.

"For about three months there was no sight of Noon Miyan. One day I remarked to my compounder, 'Hey, that man did not come any more.'

"The compounder is a cynic, like all of you. He said, 'Why should he come again? Did you believe that he would come with a lakh of rupees for you? Don't even think of it. Rather, he might just knife you if he gets an opportunity.'

"His words did not seem very illogical. Regrets at having saved the life of this murderous thug surfaced anew.

"That afternoon I was alone when Noon Miyan suddenly arrived. He no longer looked sickly, very broad and well built; saluting me enthusiastically he said, 'Huzoor![10]

"I said, 'Noor Miyan, why this sudden appearance? Have you brought your lakh rupees?'

---

10 **Huzoor**: Respectful salutation

Extracting a thick wad of notes from his lungi[11] he said, 'Malik,[12] I do not have the means of paying a lakh rupees, but have brought five thousand rupees. Please accept it and let me be debt-free.'

"Amazed I said, 'What will I do with five thousand rupees?'

"He answered, 'Huzoor, this money is my tribute. On my honour, I do not have the means to give more than this right now.'

"Smiling, I responded, 'Noor Miyan, did you think that greed for money was the reason behind my saving you?'

"Noor Miyan remained silent.

"Once again I remarked, 'The money you have brought, tainted by the sale of cocaine and sucking dry the very life force of man, I do not need. God will forgive me for the sin I have committed for saving the life of a man like you.'

"He began pleading for the money to be accepted. I did not take it. He begged me in earnest, but I remained adamant. Finally, picking up the bundle of notes, he left in a kind of huff.

"Returning after seven days Noor Miyan said, 'Malik, I just cannot forget that in spite of being a Hindu, in full knowledge, you have saved the life of an enemy like me. Fine, if you will not accept money, keep me as your slave. Whatever you command, I will do.'

An idea struck me. I asked, 'You will do whatever I say? Are you sure?'

"He said, 'On my life, on my honour–I will.'

---

11 **Lungi:** An article of clothing–a kind of ankle-length skirt worn, tied at the waist.

12 **Malik:** A respectful salutation, meaning, 'My lord'.

"Once more I asked, 'Noor Miyan, think carefully, don't just make a promise on a whim.'

"He abruptly stopped and said, 'Can't give up my religion. Besides that, I will do anything else, Khuda Kasam[13].'

"I said, 'No, I will not ask you to give up your religion. But, this is far more difficult, Noor Miyan.'

"He said, 'No matter, command me.'

"I said, 'Fine, I am commanding you to give up your cocaine business and the business of vandalism. So, will you be able to do that?'

"Noor Miyan remained as though carved in stone. With his head in his hands he was immersed in thinking God knows what. Finally, heaving a very deep sigh he said, 'Babuji, you have taken away my whole world. I will discard cocaine and vandalism. But, what do you stand to gain by this?'

"Placing my hands on his shoulders I said, 'If you can truly discard these Noor Miyan, then one day I will explain what I am gaining.'

"Noor Miyan stopped vandalism with ease. However, all that he did while attempting to give up cocaine is impossible to describe. Initially, turning up every evening he would strike his forehead against my feet. No person who has not taken cocaine will understand the demoniac craving which hunger for the drug brings. Each day he would rub his face on my feet and plead, 'Malik, give me permission just one time to take as much cocaine as one can pick on the tip of a needle. I will not take more.'

---

13 **Khoda Kasam:** God promise.

"Sometimes even I would feel sorry and I had to force myself to remain obdurate.

"But, what amazing willpower that thug had. Any other person would have forgotten all about any promise a long time back. However, like a bulldog Noor Miyan held on to his word.

"It took him one whole year to conquer that craving for cocaine. Then, once, he turned up at the end of the day and clung to my feet saying, 'Malik, today I have understood why you asked me to give up cocaine. You are not a man, but a Pir Nabi.[14]'

"Noor Miyan now has a shop of bidis[15] and tobacco. If you visit my dispensary very early, you will see Noor Miyan coming to respectfully offer his greetings the first thing every morning.'"

---

14 **Pir nabi:** Muslim holy man.
15 **Bidis:** Local hand-rolled cigarette.

The Sandalwood Idol

ONE

The image that comes to mind when we think of a Buddhist monk does not bear any similarity to an average Bengali of the present times. But, it is not just that the person about whom I am writing today, Bhikshu[1] Abhiram, was a Bengali by nationality, his appearance too was that of a typical Bengali.

It is better to clarify at the outset that it is not my intention to record in minute details a life history of Bhikshu Abhiram— and even if I wanted to, it would be impossible. I have never known the details of his lineage or nationality. Neither do I know how, being a Bengali, he had crossed into the boundaries of the Buddhist sect. I only want to put before the readers, trimming all excess and as precisely as possible, the idea I had gained of his character in only one year of acquaintance and how, the bonds of that were torn asunder for eternity one day in unthinkable circumstances. Our country is a wrestling arena of religious fervour. In the name of religion I have seen a lot of bloodshed. But, I have never before witnessed the

---

1 **Bhikshu:** A Buddhist holy man usually referred to in this manner.

strange form that the religious love of Bhikshu Abhiram took and there are very little chances that I will do so after this.

I first met Bhikshu Abhiram at the Imperial Library.[2] It is an incident, which took place about four years ago—I had just started delving into the history of the Buddhist era. In search of a rare Buddhist text, I found that he had already secured it.

Gradually I came to know him. An emaciated man with a tonsured head, the garments he supported had a saffron tinge; and he was probably below forty years of age. Bhikshu Abhiram had a very sweet manner of conversing and a smile always lingered on his lips. Just like the Udasi Sect[3] of our country, he had an uninvolved bent of mind, free from desires. But even then, he could not be disregarded as ordinary. If one looked carefully into his eyes, one realized that an intense, unquenchable desire constantly burned therein. Though he had neither tangled locks, nor was he dressed in a loin cloth, he called to mind the insane being of Rabindranath:

> Determined lips sealed in a fierce grip
> Day and night a fury in his eyes
> The twin eyes like the moth in dark
> Searching in its own light for something precise.

I had not previously imagined that a Bengali Buddhist could exist in present times, but at first sight, there had been a very strong attraction for him. Gradually the acquaintance deepened into intimacy. He started dropping in at my house

---

2 **Imperial Library:** Today, the National Library in Kolkata.
3 **Udasi Sect:** A particular religious group.

The Sandalwood Idol 99

at all odd hours. His knowledge of Buddhist History was not as deep as his knowledge of the Buddhist scriptures. So, coming to know of any new fact about Buddha's life, he would immediately inform me. There was no end to the interest he felt in my historical research; for hours on end he would listen to my lectures—his eyes burning like glow-worms.

He had no discrimination about food. Quite often when he dropped in, devoutly my wife would feed him; without a qualm he partook of fish and fowl. One day when I questioned him, with a smile he answered, "I am a Bhikshu, what is put in my bowl I will have to eat; I do not have any right to pick and choose. One day a disciple had given Tathagata[4] some pork to eat—and he had partaken even of that." The Bhikshu's eyes filled with tears all of a sudden.

After six-seven months had gone by, I came to know of something, which was the closest to his heart. A discussion on Buddhist Art was going on in my house and Bhikshu Abhiram was saying, "There are millions and millions of images of the Buddha in India and in foreign lands. But, all of them are imagined images–the manner in which the devotee artists imagined Bhagwan[5] Buddha, sculpting stone they made those images. They were not familiar with Buddha's actual form."

I said, "But I feel they were. You must have observed that almost all the images of the Buddha are the same. Of course, there are slight differences, but, overall, a common thread can

---

4 **Tathagata:** Another name for the Buddha.
5 **Bhagwan:** God, but here used as an adjective for the Buddha.

be found—large ears, curly hair and a heavy build; these can be observed in every figure. What is the reason for this? The artists must have had knowledge of his true form; They must have had a true model."

Listening attentively to all that I said, Bhikshu Abhiram remained silent for a while and then slowly he responded, "Who knows? During his lifetime, no images were made of the Buddha, sculpting was not an art form at the time. Images of the Buddha came to be widely proclaimed from the Gupta era[6], the 4th century B.C—that is almost seven hundred years after the Buddha attained Nirvana. For these seven hundred years how did man keep alive the memory of his form? Neither do the Buddhist scriptures contain any such description from which such a clear picture might be obtained. The similarity about which you are talking was probably a convention of art—initially an artist might have made an imagined image; then, through the ages, that is the likeness that has been followed." Bhikshu emitted a deep sigh, "No, man has forgotten his true image. Tutenkhamen and Amen Hotep have images of art, but there are no images of Boddhisatta's[7] bodily form."

I said, "Only those who cannot make any claims on man's memory have their own images sculpted for posterity, and not those who are truly immortal in the hearts of men. Take for example, Jesus Christ. No one knows what he actually looked like."

---

6 **Gupta era:** A particular period of time when this dynasty ruled, supposed to be an extremely.
7 **Boddhisatta:** Yest another name for the Buddha.

The Sandalwood Idol 101

He responded, "Right. Yet thousands journey and make a pilgrimage every year just to catch glimpse of a garment worn by him. If they ever got a clue about the whereabouts of his true likeness, can you imagine what their reaction would be! They would probably go mad with joy."

At this juncture my attention was suddenly drawn to his eyes. It was the look of what in English we call 'Fanatic.' The aggressive intensity which makes martyrs of men burnt in his eyes with an all-encompassing fervour. His eyes looked at me, true, but his mind-penetrating the thick mists of time of two thousand five hundred years ago seemed to be in search of that divine being's luminous image.

All of a sudden he began to speak, "Bhagwan Buddha's teeth and hair I have seen; for a few days I remained in a trance-like state of exquisite happiness. But even then, the heart was not satisfied with that. What was his physique like? What was his glance like? His powers of oration—that made an emperor discard his throne and take to the roads, a housewife discard her husband and take to the life of an ascetic; if I could hear those nectar-like words even once……."

An overwhelming emotion turned him speechless. I saw his entire body quivering with a sense of romance, unknowingly tears ran down his gaunt cheeks. I was stunned with amazement; so much emotion for so small a cause did not seem possible. I had heard that some Vaishnavites[8] immediately on hearing Krishna's[9] name, went into a kind of stupor but had not believed this. However, this emotional frenzy of

---

8 **Vaishnavites:** Followers of the God Vishnu.
9 **Krishna:** A God of the Hindu religion.

Bhiskshu did not make it seem so implausible anymore. This facet of religion I had not seen before, suddenly my eyes were opened.

Unaware of his surroundings, Bhikshu continued saying, "Gautam! Tathagata! I do not seek heavenly bliss, I do not seek heavenly bliss, I do not want Nirvana[10], just reveal your true self to me. The human body in which you traversed this world—show me that divine body, Buddha! Tathagata!"

It was clear to me that it was not Buddhism, but that great seer who had conquered him and who was responsible for this frenzy of Bhikshu.

Slowly I tiptoed out of the room. This distraught appeal, completely forgetting the self, I could not bear to see. It seemed as though I was committing an offence.

TWO

Religious fanaticism is very infectious. Probably unknowingly it had also built up in me. So, a few days after the incident referred to, turning the pages of Fa-hien's travelogue, suddenly my eyes came to a halt at one point; I almost leaped up in joy and excitement. I had read Fa-hien prior to this, why hadn't this struck me before?

Bhikshu Abhiram turned up that evening. Suppressing my agitation, I handed him the book. Curiously he asked, "What is this?"

"Read it," I said, pointing out a page. Bhikshu began reading while my eyes remained fixed on his face.

---

10 **Nirvana:** Eternal and divine fulfillment.

The Sandalwood Idol   103

"About twelve hundred cubit south of Baishali, the King of Vaishya, Sudtta, had constructed a Vihara[11] facing the south. To the left and the south of the vihara, the crystal clear waters of the pond were surrounded by innumerable trees and a variety of multi-coloured flowers, all making a gorgeous display. This was the "Jaitbon Vihara."

"When Buddha was away for religious propagation for ninety days, for his mother's welfare, Prasenjit, craving a sight of him, and using a special type of sandalwood, carved an image of him and placed it where he was usually seated. On return from Heaven, the image disregarded its own place for a meeting with the Buddha. Buddhadev then told the image, "You return to your own place; when I attain Nirvana, you will be the ideal for my students," saying which he sent back the image. This is the very first image of the Buddha and that is the model on which all subsequent models have been made.

"Some time after the Buddha had attained Nirvana, the Jaitbon Vihara was razed to the ground in a fire. All the aristocracy and their subjects were totally downcast to think that the sandalwood image had been destroyed; but five or six days later, when the doors of the small vihara were opened, the sandalwood image was seen. Joyously all decided together to reconstruct the vihara. When the first floor was built, the image was re-established in it original place..."

Like one still drowsy with sleep, Bhikshu looked at me and in low, muffled tones asked, "Where is that image?"

I answered, "Do not know. As far as I remember, I have never come across any other reference to a sandalwood image."

---

11 **Vihara:** A Buddhist monument/monastery.

After this both of us remained silent for a long time. It was apparent to me that this tiny scrap of news had caused a veritable turmoil in Bhikshu, right through his inner being. Probably I had expected some sort of spontaneous gush of happiness from him; there was also a curiosity to see how he would react to this confrontation with the unexpected. But he did nothing; after remaining still for half an hour, he suddenly stood up. In his eyes lingered that half somnolent state—not looking in any direction, as if hearing some ethereal voice, men sometimes unconsciously are led—in a similar manner he left the house.

Then for three months there was no contact with him.

Suddenly towards the middle of the month of Pous[12], like a veritable earthquake he arrived and shook my very foundations in such a manner that had been difficult to imagine even the evening before. The mere thought that even I would become involved in such a daring exploit made me cringe.

He said, "I have found a lead."

Joyously I welcomed him, "Come in, please be seated."

He did not sit, but in excited tones began to say, "I have traced it Bibhuti Babu. That image has not been lost, it is still there."

"How is that possible? Where did you locate it?"

"Have not as yet. I had gone to 'Besar'—where the ruins of ancient Baishali can still be found. Nothing remains of the Jaitbōn Vihara, except bricks and heaps of stone. But in spite of that, I have its traces in the midst of that—the image is there."

---

12 **Pous:** Month of the Bengali calendar, beginning about the middle of December.

The Sandalwood Idol

"How did you find it?"

"From one inscription on a stone block that had fallen off a dilapidated temple–this script was engraved at the back." Handing me a slip of paper and in a voice choking with emotion he said, "After the Jaitbon Vihara was destroyed, probably that temple was built using these stones; that temple too is 500-600 years old and now houses no idol. A massive banyan tree has it in its coils and is crushing its very bones—the stones are all collapsing. This script was engraved on one such stone."

Taking the paper from his hand I examined it. It was written in the Prakrit language of the 10th or the 11th century. Bhikshu had made and brought along an exact copy.

Deciphering it was not very difficult. The writing on the stone read thus–"Alas Tathagata! A great danger has befallen our religion at this time. The Jaitbon Vihara where you have spent twenty five years is in a pitiable condition. Householders no longer give alms to your followers. Royalty is antagonistic towards the Viharas. Students from different ends of the world no longer come in pursuit of studying a religion of humility. The pride and glory of Tathagata's religion is coming to an end.

"In addition we hear of a horrifying new terror. There are rumours from all around that a barbarian race known as Turks have attacked the state. They are irreligious and extremely cruel. No sooner do they see Bhikshus and other labourer, than they slaughter them heartlessly and also loot the Viharas and Sanghas[13].

---

13 **Sangha:** Habitation of the holy men of the Buddhist order.

"Hearing all these wild speculations and seeing the plight of some ailing labourers, the head of the Jaitbon Vihara, Buddharakshit Mahasaya is very disturbed. The Turks are moving in this direction and are definitely going to attack the Vihara. The inhabitants of the Vihara are pacific by nature and not at all adept in the use of arms. There are priceless jewels in the Vihara; the most invaluable of them all is the idol of the Buddha made of a special sandalwood, by Prasenjit during the lifetime of the Buddha. Who will provide protection for all this when the Turks attack?

"Mahather[14] Buddha Rakshit after reflecting continually for three days has decided on a solution. At midnight, during the coming New Moon, ten labourers of the Vihara, gathering together all the jewels and scriptures and the sandalwood idol of the Buddha will depart. About four miles (twenty jojanas) to the north of the Vihara, in a plateau of the Himalayas, there is a stone column, constructed by the demons; atop this pillar, which appears to pierce the sky, there is a secret treasure trove. It is believed that the Asuras[15] during the reign of Dharmashoka[16], Beloved of the God, had constructed this in the sensitive "Jangha[17] Region of the Himalayas. The labourers taking the sandalwood image and other precious treasures would protect them in this secret place. Once the Turkish onslaught was over, they would re-install it .

---

14 **Mahather:** Here, the head of the Vihara.
15 **Asuras:** Demons.
16 **Dharmashoka:** Ashoka, the Mighty king who was also equally known for his strong leaning towards religion and Buddhism in particular.
17 **Jangha:** High up on the Himalayas.

The Sandalwood Idol   107

"Should the Vihara be destroyed in the Turkish attack and all the inhabitants perish, in fear of this and under the instructions of Mahathir Mahasaya, for the knowledge of the coming generations, with the moon in this particular position, this writing has been engraved. May the wishes of Bhagwan Buddha be fulfilled."

The writing came to an end at this point. While reading the script, my mind too had become enmeshed in the past; the tremulous trepidation which the harmless Bhikshus of the Jaitbon Vihara had felt eight hundred years ago under the threat of danger, I could almost indistinctly visualize. The melancholy visage of the far-sighted, elderly Buddhist monk seemed to take shape before my eyes. It was as though I could envisage, for a few moments, like a cinematograph, with the help of that script, that historical junction when the fate of India faced a great threat. Terrorism throughout the country. A violent, irrepressible, impotent race! Turks! Turks! Here come the Turks! The agonized cry of millions of frightened voices began to ring in my ears.

Then I awoke from the stupor and saw a hungry jubilation in the eyes of Bhikshu. Hearing a deep sigh I said, "The purpose of the Mahasthabir Buddharakshit[18] has been fulfilled, but with so much delay!"

In vibrant tones he spoke aloud, "No matter the delay, it is still not too late. I will go, Bibhuti Babu. I will find out that monster constructed column. Have also got a few clues. I know the present name of the Upala river. Bibhuti Babu,

---

18 **Mahasthabir Buddharakshit:** The head of the Vihara as referred to previously.

one and a half thousand years ago Chinese travelers used to begin their journey from Korea, and traversing the Gobi Desert used to cross the insurmountable Himalayas and by foot reach India. Why? Only to see the motherland of the Buddha Tathagata; and knowing that within four miles lies a true likeness of Bhagwan Buddha, will we not go out in search?"

I replied, "Of course you will!"

Then, casting eyes lit with the spark of lightening on my face, he threw a tremendously powerful question at me, "Bibhuti Babu, will you not come with me?"

For a while I was dumbstruck. Go? I! Throwing aside all my work and chasing about in the hills and jungles—where would I chase after this illusive dream?

In pulsating tones Bhikshu said, "None have seen that divine image in eight hundred years. Bhagwan Sakhya Sangha has awaited us for eight hundred years atop the column—will you not go?"

I do not know what the Bhikshu's words contained. But, like a stringed instrument, reaching the peak of unbearable sweetness, the innate distaste for emerging in the outer world and the inherent tendency of the Bengali to remain ensconced at home, snapped. I stood up and grasping Bhikshu by the hand said, "I will go!"

THREE

If this epistle had been all about my thrilling Himalayan adventure, I could have, by describing innumerable exciting incidents, made the readers marvel. But, within the small

The Sandalwood Idol 109

boundaries of this story, there is no place for any excess. I have to cry a halt immediately after describing the end of our search for the demon constructed column.

Two weeks after starting out from Kolkata, the tiny hamlet we reached was at such a height and so isolated from any human habitation that one might mistake it for an eagle's eyrie in the crags of the Himalayas. We had still not reached the snowy section; but right in front, the snow-covered peaks hid one side from view. All around were naked peaks and below us hilly stones and pebbles.

Renting this stony and hard ground, the slender Upala river moved rapidly below, by the precipice. A thick coldness was all around.

There were three of us—I, Bhikshu Abhiram and a Bhutanese guide; no sooner had we drawn close to the village, when all the men, women and children surrounded us. Hardly anyone from the outside world comes here. Opening wide their slit eyes, they began to observe us.

Looking at them one would imagine them to be Lepchas or Bhutanese. There were also perhaps some traces of Aryan blood; I also saw one or two sharp and hooked noses.

Such a sharp nosed elderly person approaching us, said something in his own language, which we did not understand. Our Bhutanese guide explained that he was the head of the village and wanted to know the reason of our visit.

Simply, we expressed out purpose. Hearing everything, the man's face first of all expressed amazement and then a keen curiosity. He beckoned and took us to the village.

In a procession we moved forward. In the lead was the headman, followed by the three of us and right at the end, all the women, children and elders.

Taking us to a hut, the head seated us and noting that we were tired and thirsty, brought food and other articles for our comfort and relief. Thereafter, feeling rested and refreshed, we began conversing with the help of our Bhutanese interpreter. The sun was by then hidden in the mountains. The long Himalayan evening, as though unobserved, had been showering the clean air with a red tinge.

The headman said, about a mile to the north was a cascade–it was from that fall that the river began. That place was extremely inaccessible and excessively steep; on the other bank of the Upala, just at the mouth of the fall, was a column-like mountain peak, that is what was known all around as 'Buddhastambha'. All the villagers were in the habit of offering prayers to this Buddhastambha every full moon night. But, as the place was so unapproachable, nobody went there, they set afloat their offering on the Upala river, near the village.

Bhikshu asked, "Where is the path to cross the Upala and come closer to the Stambha?" The Headman shook his head, "True, there is a path, but it is so dangerous that none dare use it. Just below the Upala Falls, there is an ancient iron hanging chain or swinging bridge, which links the two banks. But, it has become so worn-out that men cannot cross it. Yet, that is the only path."

There was no doubt that we had reached our destination. But to be absolutely sure I asked the headman if anybody could say what that column contained. The Headman responded that while none had personally seen the contents, since time immemorial, legend had it that the Buddha himself in his own natural form resides in the column and the fragrance

The Sandalwood Idol 111

of sandal was constantly emitted; after five thousand years he would emerge, taking on the form of an ally.

Looking at me with burning eyes, Bhikshu burst out, "The Buddha himself resides in this column, the fragrance of sandal wafts from him–can you understand the meaning of the legend? Probably the labourers who had brought the image could not return, maybe they stayed behind in the village........"

The Bhikshu could not complete what he was saying. A violent tremor made our hut shake and creak loudly. We were seated on the floor, even from there a convulsion seemed to to reach out and cause a violent jerk from right below. I scrambled up,—"Earthquake!"

By the time we stood up, the tremors of the earthquake had subsided. The headman remained peacefully squatting on the floor, and observing our discomfiture with a gentle smirk informed us that there was no cause for fright; earthquakes like this happened four-five times a day, this was the region which was the birthland of the earthquake.

In stunned amazement we stared at him. The 'birthland' of the earthquake? I had never heard something of the sort before. Even then I did not know what a powerful offspring she was ready to give birth to.

Bhiskshu Abhiram, however, in great excitement cried out, "Right! Right! This is what has been referred to in the stone inscription, do you not remember?"

I could not remember where earthquakes had been referred to in the script. Bhikshu then took out from his sling bag the transcription of the writings on the stone and in jubilant tones exclaimed, "There is no further doubt, Bibhuti Babu, we have reached the right place. Here listen to this..." Saying which

112 The Scarlet Dusk

he read out a particular portion of the Prakrit[19] script. *Legend has it that the demons during the era of Dharmashoka, had constructed this in the Jangha region[20] of the Himalayas.*

I remembered. This *"susceptible to tremors'* I had thought of as a lot of poetic language. It had not occurred to me that the disguised reference might be to earthquakes. I said, "Yes, you are right—I had not taken note of that portion of the writing very carefully. This region, like Shillong, is also prone to earthquakes."

At this time my eyes fell on the headman. He had grown extremely excitable; his small slit eyes glowed and glistened, the lips quivered as if to say something. Then, stunning us, in clear Prakrit lanuage he spoke, *"Listen all, when the stars fall into a particular constellation, sunlight will be cast on the path to the stambha and make luminous the Buddha's divine body; the doors will be magically thrown open. This will consecutively happen for three days and then for a year the doors will remain closed. My beloved devotees, if you want to look on the Buddha's ethereal face and make easier the path to Nirvana, remember these words."* Saying all this in one breath, the headman began panting.

In intense amazement, Bhikshu asked, "You, you know the Prakrit language?"

Not understanding, the headman shook his head.

Then the help of the Bhutanese interpreter had to be sought. Through the interpreter the headman said that that

---

19 **Prakrit:** Written script of a India. Buddhist documents usually written using this.
20 **Jangha region:** Which is susceptible to tremors.

The Sandalwood Idol 113

was a religious incantation that was the mainstay of their religion; it had to be memorized down the generations, but he did not know the meaning. Today, hearing Bhikshu talk in that language, he had grown excited and recited that aloud.

We stared at each other.

Bhikshu told the headman, "Repeat your incantation once more."

The headman uttered the incantation aloud slowly, for the second time. I could understand everything. This was not an incantation, but instructions about entering the Buddha stambha. Thrice a year, the heat of the sunlight penetrated the cavernous path and probably heated some mechanism, as a result of which the machine operated door opened. Resorting to such mechanical devices a lot of fraudulent priests of Egypt and Assyria used to open temple doors–I remembered reading about it in books. Those responsible for the construction had been demons, that is demoniac artists; hence, controlling the entrance by such a device was not surprising. The labourers who had brought the image of the Buddha must have been aware of the secret, in case future generations forgot, they had thought of this incantation.

But, how did the headman come to know this?

I looked carefully at his face. Though the facial features were primarily Mongolian, the nostrils, eyebrows and chin had an Aryan stamp. The labours could not return; of the ten of them, one might have slipped. This headman was a descendant of that religious outcast—he had forgotten all the history of his ancestors, but like a hollow amulet, he had memorized only this basic incantation.

Awakening from the stupor, I remembered that the doors of the pillar only opened thrice a year and thereafter remained closed. When were those three days? How long would we have to wait in hopes of the door opening?

I asked Bhikshu, "When will the particular constellation they are talking about take place?"

Bhikshu took out the almanac from his bag. Examining it with full concentration for fifteen minutes, he then looked up. I saw that his lips were trembling and his eyes had filled with tears. He said, "Tomorrow is the first of Magha[21] and the sun will form that particular constellation. What a supernatural conjunction! If we had reached three days later!' His words seemed to quiver and in a choked voice full of tears he said, "Tathagata!"

My skin prickled to think of the fulfilment which would follow the all-encompassing desire. To myself I said, "Tathagata, let your Bhikshu's desires not go in vain."

FOUR

The next morning we set off in the direction of the stambha, the headman of his own accord accompanying us.

Immediately on crossing the village boundary, the path became steeply inclined. In sections the path became so steep that we had to move forward somehow, crawling on our hands and feet. There was fear of slipping and falling far below, into the ravine, at every step.

Bhikshu was speechless. His frail body seemed to possess an inexhaustible strength. He moved ahead and somehow we followed in the rear. It was as though he pulled us along on his rope of irrepressible enthusiasm.

---

21 **Magha:** A month of the Bengali calendar.

Even then we had to rest twice along the way. There was a pair of binoculars with me, I used it to examine my surroundings. Far below, the village appeared like a doll's house and all around were the lifeless, lonely mountains.

Finally, after more than three hours of a backbreaking climb of the steep incline, we reached our destination. For some time a muffled thundering sound had been heard—as if drums were playing in the distance. The headman said, "That is the noise of the fall of the Upala river."

When we went and stood at the edge of the fall, the exquisite beauty that lay in front stunned us and turned us motionless for a moment. About fifty yards above from where we were standing, the foaming torrents of the Upala appeared to spring into space through a narrow channel.

Then, like a curved rainbow falling two hundred feet below, in a wayward and uncontrolled violent motion, creating a vortex, she flowed away. Just like water which arises from a boiling cauldron, the foaming torrential waters breaking through the boulders seemed to strike us in the face like a shower of rain.

At this point there was a gap of almost fifty yards between the two banks. It appeared as though the mountain had had been ripped asunder to throw open the exit for the pebbles and stones. It was frightening to see the frail bridge constructed by weak humans to link this impassable ravine. Two iron chains, one above and the other below–ran parallel from one bank to the other. This was the bridge. The frail, rusted iron chains in the background of the roaring waterfall seemed to be even more fragile than a spider's web—even a slight breeze would snap it in two.

But I have not yet talked of the other bank. The appearance of nature on the other side was absolutely different. Perhaps due to temperamental diversity, Mother Nature had separated them. If one suddenly happened to look across, it would seem as though the entire area was full of pillars. As far as the eye extended, oval hillocks, small-medium-big were scattered here and there. Those who have seen the Dhamek Stupa at Sarnath will have some idea of what the deep ravine was like. A beautiful pillar, like a slender minar[22] ascended in an upward direction. Its stone body glistened in the afternoon sunlight. Looking at it one would suspect that like the demon Moy[23], some being from the other world, with a lot of care had constructed this divine column and left it behind.

This was a creation made during the childhood of the earth, when Nature was still engrossed in her playhouse. Maybe man too played some part in its construction. I carefully looked with the binocular, but the exterior revealed sign of the hand of man. There was no way to make out from the outside that the column was hollow; only a tiny opening at the peak of the column caught my eye—it was quadrangular and would not be more than a cubit in length and breadth. The rays of sunlight filtered through that opening on to the path. This must be the opening mentioned in the incantation.

Engrossed, I was imbibing the sight. Suddenly looking to the side, I saw Bhikshu, completely stretched out on the ground, respectfully saluting the Buddha.

---

22 **Minar:** A tall pillar like structure usually well decorated and dedicated to something particular.
23 **Moy:** The manufacturing Engineer of the Demon Tribes.

The Sandalwood Idol 117

Bhikshu Abiram did not listen to us and alone, he used the iron chain to cross over to the other side. The three of us remained on the other side. At each step the fright grew—perhaps the chain would snap any moment. But Bhikshu was lean and slight–it did not break.

Reaching the other side, Bhikshu waved to reassure us and then moved towards the column. Having surveyed the column once, he once again raised his hands and shouted out something; but in the noise of the cascade, we could not hear. It seemed that he had found the door of the column open.

Then he entered and we could not see him any more. I sat there with the binoculars fixed to my eyes. I used my mind's eyes to see—in the darkness Bhikshu slowly climbed the circular steps; in trembling, indistinct tones perhaps the incantation was spoken aloud, *"Tathagata, Tamasa Ma Jyotir Gamaya"*[24]

Was that special sandalwood idol still there? I could not see it; but there were no regrets because of that. If that statue was there, later forces could be brought and it could be rescued. A furore would break out through the country.

Ten minutes went by.

Then, everything turned upside down. Suddenly the Himalayas appeared to turn insane. The ground began to tremble. From the bowels of the earth a muffled groaning rose, like the death throes of a demon's shriek. The iron chain snapped and like a whip struck both banks.

---

24 **Tamasa Ma Jyotir Gamaya**: Buddha, bring me from darkness into light.

I will not describe any further that earthquake of the first of Magha. Only, allow me to say this much –those who have witnessed this earthquake in the plains of India cannot even imagine the condition of the birthplace of the earthquake.

Why we did not die I do not know; probably because our life-span still remained. The frenzied dancing of the earth— we collapsed on to it. In front of our eyes, the column swayed like the mast of a ship battered by the wind. As though in a senseless stupor we gazed in that direction.

Suddenly a shadow of worry was cast on my mind.

Bhikshu! What would happen to Bhikshu?

The intensity of the earthquake lessened somewhat. It seemed as if it was coming to an end. The binoculars were clutched in my fist, I brought it to my eyes. It was useless to run away and so I did not even attempt to do so.

Once again the earthquake started with renewed vigour; as if regretting the momentary lapse, it grew a hundred times more ferocious and would not rest till the earth had been destroyed.

But Bhikshu?

So far the column had been swaying like a mast, but it could withstand no longer; it broke into two from the base. The column tottered on the brink of the bottomless ravine for a while and then, like one crazed with the thought of death, plunged into the ravine. From the far depths below, a tremendous spray of foam arose and hid the column from view.

While the column had been swaying in an undecided manner at the edge of the ravine, for a split second I had seen Bhikshu. The binoculars were of course held to my eyes. I saw Bhikshu standing in the passage, with the sunlight falling on his face. A heavenly joy flooded his face. He was completely unaware of the catastrophic disaster all around.

I did not see him anymore. The death crazed column plunged into the ravine.

I returned home alone.

A few years have passed since then, but I have been unable to share the story with anybody. Whenever I think of Bhikshu, an agonizing pain pierces my heart.

But I console myself with the thought that the absolute desire of his heart had not remained unfulfilled. What wondrous image of the Buddha had risen before his eyes I do not know, but there was no doubt that the reason around which his life had centred, had attained fruition. I can see even today the ethereal joy on his face at the moment of death.

24th Asad 1343